Captive at Kangaroo Springs

Books by Robert Elmer

ADVENTURES DOWN UNDER

#1 / *Escape to Murray River*
#2 / *Captive at Kangaroo Springs*
#3 / *Rescue at Boomerang Road*

THE YOUNG UNDERGROUND

#1 / *A Way Through the Sea*
#2 / *Beyond the River*
#3 / *Into the Flames*
#4 / *Far From the Storm*
#5 / *Chasing the Wind*
#6 / *A Light in the Castle*
#7 / *Follow the Star*
#8 / *Touch the Sky*

ROBERT ELMER

CAPTIVE AT KANGAROO SPRINGS

BETHANY HOUSE PUBLISHERS
MINNEAPOLIS, MINNESOTA 55438

Captive at Kangaroo Springs
Copyright © 1997
Robert Elmer

008171

Cover illustration by Chris Ellison
Cover design by Peter Glöege

Scripture quotations identified KJV are from the King James Version of the Bible.

Published by Bethany House Publishers
A Ministry of Bethany Fellowship, Inc.
11300 Hampshire Avenue South
Minneapolis, Minnesota 55438

Printed in the United States of America.

Library of Congress Cataloging-in-Publication Data

Elmer, Robert.
    Captive at Kangaroo Springs / by Robert Elmer.
        p. cm. — (Adventures down under ; 2)
    Summary: In Australia, having settled with their family in a kind but mysterious riverboat captain's shantyhouse, twelve-year-old Patrick and his older sister, Becky, are captured by bushrangers.
    ISBN 1–55661–924–3 (pbk.)
    [1. Robbers and outlaws—Fiction. 2. Australia—Fiction.] I. Title.
II. Series: Elmer, Robert. Adventures down under ; 2.
PZ7.E4794Cap   1997
[Fic]—dc21

                                  97–21035
                                      CIP
                                        AC

To John King

. . . friend and fellow writer.

MEET ROBERT ELMER

ROBERT ELMER is the author of THE YOUNG UNDERGROUND series, as well as many magazine and newspaper articles. He lives with his wife, Ronda, and their three children, Kai, Danica, and Stefan (and their dog, Freckles), in a Washington State farming community just a bike ride away from the Canadian border.

CONTENTS

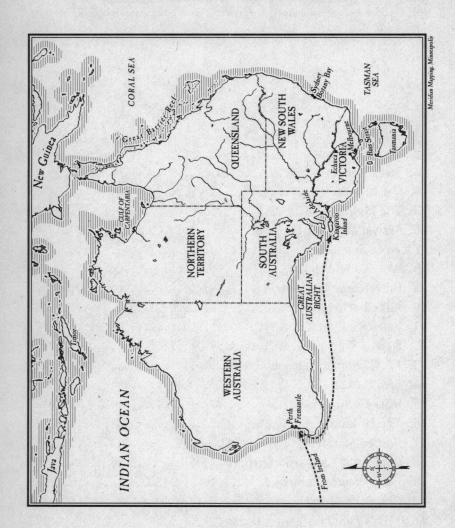

CORAL SEA

New Guinea

Great Barrier Reef

GULF OF
CARPENTARIA

QUEENSLAND

NEW SOUTH
WALES

Sydney
Botany Bay

TASMAN
SEA

NORTHERN
TERRITORY

SOUTH
AUSTRALIA

Adelaide

Echuca
VICTORIA
Melbourne

0 Bass Strait

Tasmania

Kangaroo
Island

Java

Timor

INDIAN OCEAN

WESTERN
AUSTRALIA

GREAT
AUSTRALIAN
BIGHT

Perth
Fremantle

From Ireland

W · S · E · N

Meridian Mapping, Minneapolis

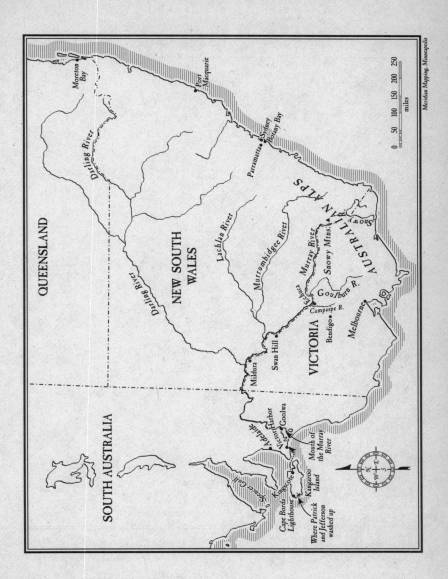

QUEENSLAND

SOUTH AUSTRALIA

NEW SOUTH WALES

VICTORIA

AUSTRALIAN ALPS

Darling River

Darling River

Lachlan River

Murrumbidgee River

Murray River

Goulburn R.

Campaspe R.

Snowy Mtns.

Snowy

Moreton Bay

Port Macquarie

Parramatta
Sydney
Botany Bay

Mildura

Swan Hill

Bendigo

Melbourne

Adelaide

Goolwa

Victor Harbor

Mouth of the Murray River

Spencer Gulf

Kingscote

Cape Borda Lighthouse

Kangaroo Island

Where Patrick and Jefferson washed up

Echuca

0 50 100 150 200 250
miles

Meridian Mapping, Minneapolis

CHAPTER 1

WANTED!

Twelve-year-old Patrick McWaid stood on his tiptoes and gaped at the latest issue of the *Riverine Herald*, tacked on the newspaper office door.

"It doesn't even sound like him," agreed his sister, Becky. She had turned fifteen a month earlier but was petite and almost a head shorter than Patrick. "And the name . . ."

They heard footsteps coming down the plank sidewalk toward them, and she lowered her voice. "The name isn't even spelled right."

"M-c-Q-u . . ." Patrick crossed his arms and read the large notice once more as people passed behind them. Their father's name, John McWaid, was splashed across the top in big letters under the headline: "Dangerous Escaped Prisoner Reported in Echuca Area."

" 'Escaped from Her Majesty's prison ship the *Hougoumont*, January 1868,' " Becky continued reading in a low voice, " 'after having been transported from his home in Dublin, Ireland, for violent criminal acts.' "

"Who would have written that, Becky? 'Violent criminal acts'?"

As she studied the notice, Becky put a hand to her chin and took a step back, narrowly avoiding a large mud puddle.

"I don't know, either, Patrick. But look there, it tells how at first they thought he had died, but that he was later discovered to have escaped from the prison in Western Australia on another ship."

"How do they know all that?" wondered Patrick.

Becky shook her head. "It also says he disappeared again by the time they made it to Adelaide, near the mouth of this river. Says here he's 'extremely dangerous.'"

"Dangerous, ha." Patrick scowled at his reflection in the glass window in front of him. His deep green Irish eyes seemed to sparkle when he was mad, and he ignored the curious stare of a man sitting behind a desk inside the newspaper office. "About as dangerous as we are."

Patrick ran his hand through his fire red hair before turning away from the newspaper office. He had liked the bustling river town of Echuca the first time he saw it two weeks ago. Maybe it was the way the river wrapped around the center of the eager frontier town. Never mind that the streets turned to mud every time it rained, and half the houses were just simple bark-and-shingle huts. The other half were grand-looking brick or wood-frame stores and hotels, and the tall wharf was proudly piled with crates of supplies and bales of wool from the outlying farms. But today everything just looked dreary, muddy, and wet. In May it was autumn down under in Australia.

"Wait a minute, Patrick." Becky pointed at the newspaper. "Did you see where it says he's been reported coming this way, up the Murray River to Echuca?"

"I saw it."

"And that fits with what Pa said in the letter, doesn't it?"

The letter Pa had written to their grandfather. Patrick patted his back pocket, as he had dozens of times before, just to make sure it was still there. Becky had told him he would ruin it by carrying it around so much. But somehow it just felt better to keep it in his pocket, the same way he kept the ring that had once belonged to his grandmother on a string around his neck.

"It all makes sense, Patrick," his sister continued in a softer voice as they jumped from plank to plank along the bog of mud called High Street. "If Pa said in the letter he would try to meet up with our grandfather here, then it must be him people have seen, don't you think?"

"Maybe." Patrick had a headache from trying to figure it out. "But if he doesn't know *we're* here, what's going to keep him from going back home to Ireland once he figures out our grandfather isn't here?"

"I don't know. What did we expect?"

Patrick sighed. They had been through the same conversation before, over and over again. "I guess I was hoping we'd just come up the river here to Echuca and knock on a couple of doors. We'd find our long-lost grandpa, he would help us find Pa, then help us prove he's not guilty."

"And we'd all live happily ever after. . . ." Becky looked down while Patrick kicked a pebble as hard as he could into a puddle.

"But now everyone knows about Pa," he complained. "And even if we *do* find him, they'll throw him back in prison, like they did back home in Ire—"

The sound of a shrill steam whistle down at the wharf cut off his last word. *Ireland. The other side of the world.*

"I don't know, Patrick." Becky pulled up the hem of her long gingham dress and turned the corner. "But I'm going to go see if Ma is still shopping here in town."

"Go ahead. I'll be back down at the wharf."

Their mother had been in town all that Friday morning, buying supplies for the crew of the paddle steamer *Lady Elisabeth*—the one that had brought them to Echuca. "Running errands for you is the least we can do to repay you for letting us stay on board these past two weeks," she had told the captain of the *Lady E*, as some of the locals called it. Everyone called the captain "the Old Man," but no one could explain why he didn't use his real name. No one could explain very much else about him, for that matter.

"Michael?" Patrick called as he picked his way around some bales of wool and climbed down the ladder from the wharf to the deck of the steamer. The tops of the proud ship's twin smokestacks floated barely even with the wharf. Even though the rains had already started, there still was not enough runoff water in the river to bring them up to eye level.

"Michael? You'd better still be here." Patrick checked the wheelhouse for signs of his eight-year-old brother. He skipped through the main salon, or sitting room, then the little closetlike room where his mother and Becky slept, the galley, and the captain's quarters. No Michael.

Patrick guessed his brother could have been off fishing or picking eucalyptus tree leaves to feed his baby koala, Christopher. But Michael had promised not to leave the boat while Patrick and Becky were gone.

"You're going to be in trouble, Michael." Patrick stood on the deck with his hands on his hips and looked around at the muddy river flowing by, less than a hundred yards to the opposite shore. Three other paddle steamers were tied up at the wharf, too. When he heard voices back up on the wharf, he could tell one of them was his mother's.

"I beg your pardon, sir, but how would I have seen my husband, considering . . ."

Patrick crawled slowly up the ladder to the wharf, peeking over the edge just enough to see the back of a tall, gray-haired man in a rounded black helmet and a police uniform with a tall collar. If Patrick had wanted to, he could have reached out and almost grabbed the cuff of the man's black trousers. Sarah McWaid faced the constable, her arms full of parcels. A couple of dock workers unloading a cart curiously glanced their way.

"And I presume you've read the latest *Riverine Herald*?" Patrick knew right away the man meant the notice about their father.

"I've seen it, sir." Mrs. McWaid lowered her eyes, and her cheeks flushed.

"Well, then I must tell you that we've received additional reports that the escaped felon—I'm referring of course to your husband—has been seen on board the *Lady Elisabeth*."

Mrs. McWaid gasped. "That's nonsense. Who would say such a thing?"

"I'm not at liberty to reveal that just now." He spoke slowly, almost as if apologizing.

The words sent a chill up Patrick's spine.

"But, sir, if someone says they saw John, then surely I should be entitled to know more. It's simply not true."

"All the same, I can only tell you that our source is considered reliable and quite detailed in his description. So I must remind you that harboring an escaped felon is an extremely serious offense."

"Of course, but we haven't—"

"And if you were discovered to be aiding this prisoner, even if he is your husband, you would be subject to arrest and imprisonment. Now . . ."

"Hey, Patrick, what are you looking at?" came a loud voice from the deck of the *Lady Elisabeth*. "Can I see?"

Michael. *Where did he come from?* Patrick ducked and waved his hand to silence his brother, but it was already too late.

"Quiet, Michael!" he hissed as he tried desperately to lower himself down the ladder.

"You, boy!" boomed the constable's voice at the top of the ladder. "Come up here."

Patrick had no choice but to climb back up the ladder and join his mother. Michael was right on his heels.

"Thanks a lot," Patrick whispered to his brother before they faced the constable.

"For what?" asked Michael.

"Doing a little spying, lad?" The constable grinned at him.

"These are my two boys," put in Mrs. McWaid. "I'm sure they meant no harm."

The constable held up his hand, and Patrick swallowed hard.

"No, I'm sure they didn't." He crouched down awkwardly in front of Michael. "My name's Constable Fitzgerald. And you are?"

"I'm Michael," answered Patrick's brother, never taking his eyes off the man. "He's Patrick."

"Well, Michael and Patrick." Constable Fitzgerald straightened out again. "Did you happen to hear what I was telling your mother?"

Michael shook his head. "I was hiding with my pet koala, Christopher, when Patrick was looking for me. I could show him to you. He's sleeping now, but you could see him."

"Hiding, were you?" The constable seemed interested. "Well, now, I'd be glad to see your pet some other time. Right now, though, I was just wondering how your father was doing. Is he well?"

Patrick understood the man was hoping for information, but Michael's innocent eyes grew wide. "You know our father?"

"Not personally, but I've heard all about him. Can you tell me where to find your father?"

"It's a secret. We don't know, either."

Constable Fitzgerald frowned and finally turned his attention to Patrick.

"Listen, lad, we're going to locate him eventually, and it would be far better for everyone concerned if it were sooner rather than later."

Patrick bit his lip but said nothing.

"Ahh, never mind." Constable Fitzgerald paused before turning back to their mother. "Now, you boys understand that it's against the law to harbor an escaped prisoner. A serious crime. And under the law . . ."

Mrs. McWaid waited stiffly. "Pardon me, constable, but I'm sure the boys have no desire to break any laws."

"Yes, well . . ." The constable frowned. "I think you know what I'm trying to say. Now, if you please, Mrs. McWaid, you will come with me. I'll need to ask you a few more questions."

CHAPTER 2

THE COVER-UP

"He took your mother *where*?" The Old Man nearly exploded when Becky, Patrick, and Michael told him the story nearly two hours after their mother had been taken away.

"She told us to stay here and wait for you to get back," explained Becky, her eyes puffy and swollen from crying. "I was just walking back to the wharf when the constable took her away to the police station."

"Of all the ridiculous stories." The Old Man started out the door. "Escaped convicts on the *Lady Elisabeth*, did he say?"

"That's what he said," Patrick told him.

"Well, then, let me go set things straight," he promised. "Alex Fitzgerald may be doing his job, but this has gone too far. You three stay on the boat."

The Old Man slammed the door behind him and was gone. They looked at each other for a moment before Becky disappeared into her tiny room and Michael went to find Christopher. After a few minutes of staring at the river, Patrick wandered out on deck.

Stay here on the boat? Patrick thought glumly. *Not again.*

From somewhere above he heard the screeching laugh of the kookaburra, a squat bird with a large, powerful beak.

"Ha-ha-ha," screeched the kookaburra, but Patrick still couldn't tell where the bird perched.

"It's not funny," he told the bird. When he looked up again, a loop of rope dropped over his head and tightened around his waist.

"Gotcha!" exclaimed someone up on the wharf, and for a moment the voice sounded just like the kookaburra's laugh.

Patrick looked up to see a boy about his own age, maybe a year or two older, grinning from ear to ear and holding tightly to his end of the rope. He looked tanned to the bone, wiry, and muscled. At least from below, he looked much taller than Patrick, and his knees poked through his pants as if he had been doing a lot of growing.

"What do you think you're doing?" yelled Patrick, trying to get free.

The other boy held his ground, then tied his rope off to a post on the wharf and slid down hand under hand. He landed in a heap on the deck, knocking Patrick down in the process.

"Name's John Henry Duggan, but my mates call me Jack." The boy jumped to his feet and held out his hand, but Patrick still couldn't move his arms away from his sides. John Henry Duggan grinned and shook Patrick's hand anyway, which was dangling helplessly. Feeling like a rag doll, Patrick tried not to wince beneath the crushing grip.

"I'm Patrick Mc—" Patrick caught his breath, remembering his father's description in the newspaper. *John McWaid, Dangerous Escaped Prisoner*. He couldn't tell anyone, at least not yet.

"Pleased to meet you, Patrick Mick." Jack looked around the *Lady Elisabeth* but made no move to untie Patrick. "So how do you like the lasso?"

"Works fine." Patrick wiggled his arms. "But . . ."

"Learned it from an American from California named Rogers. He had a traveling Wild West show that came to town, and I sneaked in the back. Watched him do the rope trick ten times. Want to see what else I can do?"

"I'd like to see you untie me."

Jack took a deep breath, cupped his hands to his mouth, and let loose with the *ha-ha-ha* bird call.

"That was you!" Patrick finally wiggled free of his noose. "I thought it was a real bird."

"'Course you did, mate." Jack squinted at Patrick, as if seeing him for the first time. "So, what are you doing on my boat?"

"*Your* boat?" Patrick straightened and stood his ground. Even though the other boy was built like a wrestler, Patrick was in no mood to back away.

"That's right, Irish boy." Jack patted Patrick on the back as if he had known him for years. "I've captured every boat that ever tied up at the Echuca wharf. Then I let the grown-ups borrow them, if they ask nice and polite."

Patrick threw the lasso to the deck, crossed his arms, and frowned. "How did you know I'm Irish?"

Jack Duggan peered at Patrick more closely, like a doctor examining a patient. "You're no gum sucker, that's for sure. And if you don't know what you sound like, you're not as smart as I thought."

Gum sucker? Patrick made a mental note to find out what the name meant as he heard footsteps coming out on deck.

"Well, look who's here," said Jack. "The boy with the koala."

When they stood next to each other, it was obvious that Michael McWaid was Patrick's brother, only he had a thicker crop of freckles on his cheeks and was four years younger. Michael held a bundle of gray fur in his arms and looked uncertainly at the boys on the deck of the paddle steamer.

"Is Ma back yet?" asked Michael.

Patrick shook his head.

"Your little brother, isn't he? What happened to your older brother?"

Patrick looked at the other boy sideways. "His name is Michael, and I don't have an older brother."

"Yes, you do. A taller fellow? I saw him on the wharf with you the other day."

"Oh, you probably mean Jefferson Pitney. He isn't our brother. He's a cabin boy on the ship that brought us to Australia. Had to go back to his ship the day before yesterday."

"But he's coming back as soon as he can," began Michael. "He promised he'd help us look for our . . ."

Patrick shook his head fiercely to keep his brother from saying "Pa." Christopher the koala turned his little head and stared at them with sleepy black eyes, and Jack poked curiously at the little animal.

"Your what?"

"Nothing," answered Patrick. "Nothing at all."

"Oh, come on," Jack persisted. "He was going to say something."

Patrick just crossed his arms stubbornly until Jack threw up his hands in defeat.

"All right. But what's wrong with your animal? He looks half dead."

"He mostly sleeps during the day," explained Michael, finding a place for Christopher in the paddle steamer's salon. He made sure the sleepy animal was safely inside, then closed the door and followed the other boys up to the wheelhouse.

"I thought all gum suckers would know about koalas." Patrick challenged the visitor.

"What's a gum sucker, Patrick?" asked Michael.

"You know what a gum tree is?" Jack puffed out his chest. "Gum sucker means a native born in Victoria State, Australia. Like me."

"I was born in Dublin, Ireland," volunteered Michael. "Now we live on this boat."

"That so?" Jack raised his eyebrows. "Then you and your brother probably know all kinds of things about paddle steamers."

Michael crossed his arms proudly. "Ask us anything."

Jack thought for a moment, then looked up at a tiny certificate hanging on the wall behind them. "What's the Old Man's real name?"

"You're taller than we are," answered Patrick. "You read it. That certificate probably shows his name."

"No." Jack looked down and scuffed the floorboards with his toe. "I mean, I don't read . . . uh . . . so good."

Patrick studied the older boy. "You can't read? Really?"

"You heard me the first time. Just tell me what it says."

"Sorry." Patrick leaned over a chart table and stood on his tiptoes to read the certificate. "It says 'New England Harbor Pilots Association.' Hmmm . . ."

"What's the name?" asked Michael.

Patrick reached down to steady himself and stretched a little more.

"Here, it says . . . whoa!"

Something slipped under Patrick's hands as he leaned for support. Before he realized what was happening, he fell face-first onto the chart table, ripping his way through a scroll-like chart of the river that was stretched between two rollers.

"Oh no!" he gasped, staring at the ruined chart.

"Now you've really done it," said Jack. He pulled Patrick away from the accident. "You know how valuable these things are?"

Patrick groaned and ran a hand through his hair. "I have to tell the Old Man what happened. Maybe he can fix it."

"Don't be stupid." Jack looked closely at the mess Patrick had made of the charts. "I hear the Old Man has already killed three men. Tied 'em up in a sack and tossed 'em out in the river, just like he'll do to you if he finds out what you did."

"Three men?" Patrick didn't believe it, but . . .

"How do you know?" Michael questioned.

Jack rolled his eyes as if everyone on the river should know. "You've been living on this paddle steamer, and you don't know? Everyone knows about the Old Man's temper."

Patrick stared at the ruined river chart, frozen with fear. "We can't just leave it like this," he squeaked.

" 'Course not." The older boy picked up one end of the rolled chart and tucked it under the other. "Just slip 'em back together, like so. Now roll it up."

"I don't know. . . ." Patrick slowly rolled up the chart until the ripped part was hidden, folded back into the roll. "Won't he—"

"Quit worrying." Jack wadded up a ruined section of the map and tossed it out the side door into the river, where the current drifted it away. "It'll be days before he finds out, and he'll probably think he did it himself. You're going to thank me for saving you like this."

"That's sneaky!" complained Michael.

"It wouldn't be right," Patrick added weakly.

Jack shook his head from side to side and put his hand on his hip.

"It's up to you. But if you ask me, he's—"

"He's coming!" interrupted Michael. The boat rocked slightly as the Old Man jumped aboard from the wharf and started up the ladder to the wheelhouse.

"Remember his temper," Jack told them seconds before the door swung open.

"Jack Duggan." The Old Man stepped into the wheelhouse with a frown on his face. "Up to trouble again, are you?"

"Where's Ma?" asked Michael. "Did you see her?"

Becky must have heard them talking; Patrick noticed her staring curiously up at the wheelhouse from the deck below.

"Is Ma coming back?" she called up at them.

"I was just leaving," said Jack, backing away toward the other door. "I'll talk to you later, Patrick Mick."

Jack ducked out the door and slid down the ladder, landing with a sweep of his hands at Becky's feet. Using a nearby rowboat as a springboard, he hopscotched to the deck of another paddle steamer but was shooed away from that boat by a man wearing an apron and waving a wooden spoon.

"Your mother's fine," the Old Man finally answered Becky's question. He watched Jack carefully until the boy disappeared up on the wharf. "She'll be right along."

"But what happened with the constable?" Becky climbed up to join them.

The Old Man dismissed her worry with a wave of his hand. "Ah, just a lot of nonsense. Foolish questions." He faced Patrick and Michael with a stern glare. "And speaking of foolishness, what were you boys doing up here? How long was that larrikin Jack Duggan on board my paddle steamer?"

"I have to go check on Christopher," said Michael, tripping

backward from where he stood next to the big steering wheel. "I think it's time for his dinner."

"I'll help you," added Becky, and she disappeared down the ladder as quickly as she had come.

Patrick was left alone to face the Old Man's stare.

"I'm not sure what a larrikin is," replied Patrick, his back to the charts. "But he was here just a few minutes." He felt with his hand to make sure the rollers were straight.

"Larrikin. A troublemaker, sure as you're born. Soon as you turn your head he and his mates will jump on any paddle steamer at the wharf as if they own it."

Patrick took a deep breath, and the blood pounded in his ears. "Actually, sir, there's something I need to tell you. . . ."

"Eh?" The Old Man studied him with a raised eyebrow, and Patrick instantly changed his mind. The words seemed to stick to the roof of his mouth.

"Uh . . ." Patrick shivered and tried to think. "We'll make sure we keep larrikins off the boat from now on."

The Old Man looked around to where Patrick was holding his hands behind his back.

"That what you had to say?"

"No, sir—I mean, yes, sir."

"You hiding anything back there?"

"No, sir." Patrick shook his head violently and held out his empty hands in front of him. "Nothing. But I'd better go help Michael feed his koala, too."

"That youngster is needing a lot of help, all of a sudden," mumbled the Old Man.

Patrick held on to the sides of the ladder and flew down to the deck in one giant leap, the way he had seen Jack Duggan do. The wood burned the palms of his hands, and he hit the lower deck so hard he crumpled to his knees.

"Ow!" he cried, pain shooting through his right ankle.

"Are you all right, Patrick?"

Patrick looked up to see his mother looking down at him from the wharf.

"Ma! You're back."

"Of course I'm back," she told him as she stepped carefully down the ladder. "But it looks as if you're trying to hurt yourself."

Patrick quickly pulled himself up and limped across the deck to give her a hand. "Never mind me, Ma. We were worried about *you*."

Mrs. McWaid collapsed into a chair when they stepped into the salon, and Michael and Becky crowded around.

"Someone has convinced the constable that we know something about your father's whereabouts," she told them quietly, putting her arms around her children. "I only wish we did."

The Old Man slipped in and cleared his throat.

"Oh, Captain," began Mrs. McWaid. "Thank you so much for talking to the police—"

"No need to thank me, Mrs. McWaid. But now here's what we'll do: As soon as we can arrange it, I want you to go stay in my shanty just up the river, until I get back."

"But, Captain, we couldn't—"

"Nonsense, it's settled. I'm warning you, it's not much, and I suppose it needs a woman's touch. Still, it's a little ways out of town, out of the way. You'll be safer there."

"Safer than what?" asked Michael.

"Safer, that's all." The Old Man frowned and continued talking to their mother. "You didn't tell the constable about your letter, did you?"

Mrs. McWaid shook her head. "He didn't ask."

"Of course he didn't ask. How would he know?" He held out his hand to Patrick. "Here, let me see it again, lad."

Patrick pulled the letter from his father out of his pocket and placed it gingerly in the Old Man's hand. The grizzled sailor held it at arm's length, squinted, and studied it carefully.

"Tell me once more how you came upon this?"

"At the post office," Patrick explained, pointing to the name on the envelope. "See, it's addressed to my grandfather, but his name is Patrick McWaid, too, so they thought it was for me."

"But I don't think our grandfather has been here in Echuca," added Becky. "No one's ever heard of him."

The Old Man nodded. "All right. Now, listen here, Mrs. McWaid. If your husband is still searching for his father the way he says he is in this letter, there's a chance he might learn you're here, too."

Mrs. McWaid nodded. "What are you saying we should do?"

The Old Man shook his head. "I'm only saying there's a chance. If he does find you, I want you to stay in my shanty, keep quiet, and wait for me to return. Understand?"

Everyone nodded seriously as he continued his instructions.

"I'm heading up the river day after tomorrow for a quick delivery before we turn around for the run back down to Goolwa. I'll be passing through Echuca again in a few days."

"Do you really think my father will find us?" asked Becky.

"I didn't say that, Miss Becky." The Old Man held up his hands. "But you'd better hope he does—before someone else finds *him*."

CHAPTER 3

STICK GAMES

Saturday afternoon on Echuca wharf was as busy as any weekday. Dozens of men loaded and unloaded their paddle steamers while the steam engines puffed and cranes twirled in an odd dance by the river. Patrick and Michael kept watch from inside the salon of the *Lady Elisabeth*.

"Let's go up to the wheelhouse, Patrick," suggested Michael. "We can see better from up there."

Patrick could hear the Old Man's voice upstairs shouting at a crew of three or four men who were struggling with a load of wool on the forward deck.

"I'm not going up there. Let's go up on the wharf and watch the stick game instead."

"What's that?"

"Stick. You know that game the fellows all play."

Michael shook his head.

"Look." Patrick took a broomstick and sat down. "You sit down there, in front of me, but facing me."

Michael did as his brother told him.

"Now you put the soles of your feet right up against mine, and you grab the broomstick with both hands, one on each end so it's sideways. See?"

"But I can't reach it."

"Bend your knees, then, just a little. Then when I say, you pull the stick and try to pull me so I'm standing up. I do the same thing. Whoever pulls the other one up wins."

"That's silly, Patrick. I can't do that."

"Why not?"

"I told you. My arms aren't long enough."

Patrick frowned and stood up. "Well, let's go watch, then."

He felt his tender right ankle once more when he jumped out on the wharf, but Patrick tried not to limp as they walked up to a group of spectators around the stick contest. The boys, most of them in their teens, cheered at the action as they huddled between two piles of wooden freight boxes, just above where the *Lady Elisabeth* was moored. No one looked up.

"Pull, Jack," urged one of the boys.

"Come on, Dawson!" yelled another.

Patrick had to stand on his tiptoes to see over their shoulders, but he could hear the grunting. In the middle of the ring sat a red-faced boy, feet to feet with Jack Duggan and locked in a furious contest.

"Lift me up, Patrick," said Michael, who had trotted up from behind. A couple of the boys looked back in surprise.

"Well, if it isn't the kid with the koala and his big brother," said one. "Here to try your hand?"

Patrick just shook his head and watched. The boy named Dawson wasn't giving up, but his cheeks puffed with every tug and pull. Jack was red-faced, too, but he seemed to be doing most of the pulling.

"Come on, Dawson!" yelled Michael, making fists and pulling as if he were in the contest, too.

In the next moment, it was all over. Jack leaned backward with a mighty grunt and pulled his opponent to his feet, the same way Patrick had tried to show his younger brother a few minutes before. Most of the crowd cheered; only a few groaned.

"Right-oh!" puffed Jack. He held the stick high and allowed two of his friends to lift him to his feet. "Any of you other blokes like to have a go now?"

"Aww," said one, waving his hand. "You know none of us can beat you. Not even two at a time."

Jack chuckled as he caught his breath. "How 'bout you, Irish boy?"

Patrick held up his hand. "Not me. I'm just watching."

But Jack looked him straight in the eye. "All right, so I'll make you a bargain."

The crowd hushed as they looked at the newcomers. Patrick's mouth went dry.

"What kind of bargain? I don't have any money."

The older boy shook his head and wiped his hands on his pants legs.

"Not talking about money. You win, and I'll keep your little secret. I win, and you tell me the Old Man's real name. You never told me before. Fair?"

"Ha!" said one of the other boys. "This one's going to be too easy."

"You wouldn't . . ." began Patrick, but he felt every eye on him.

"You don't want to get in a stick contest with that fellow," said the boy named Dawson. "He cheats."

Patrick didn't listen, only sat down and matched his feet up with Jack's. He tried to ignore the pain in his ankle that throbbed every time he put pressure on it.

"This is going to be a quick one, boys," Jack told his friends.

Patrick reached out for the stick.

"You can do it, Patrick," piped up Michael. Patrick could always count on his little brother to cheer him on.

"Go ahead and pull," Jack said after Patrick had been tugging for at least a minute. The other boys shouted for Jack while only Michael cheered for Patrick.

He's much stronger than I am, thought Patrick. *But maybe he's getting tired.*

"I haven't heard any shouting from the Old Man yet," grunted Jack.

"Shouting?"

"You know what I'm talking about. I haven't told him yet about what you did."

Patrick pulled and twisted, but the bigger boy matched every move. Jack was toying with him, and he knew it. The pain shot through Patrick's ankle every time he pressed to the right.

"I'll bet he knows already," Patrick blurted out.

"If he did, you wouldn't still be alive. I guarantee it."

"Well, he *will* know." Patrick pulled again, but Jack was a brick wall. "I'm going to tell him what happened."

Jack just stared at Patrick.

"You're crazy," said the older boy. "Why would anyone want to confess to the Old Man? I told you what he'll do to you."

"Doesn't matter," Patrick grunted back. "I'm going to tell him before you do."

For just a moment Jack's mouth hung slack, as if he still couldn't understand what Patrick had just told him. Patrick leaned back and pulled with all his strength. Jack popped to his feet, and the crowd groaned.

"Hey!" Patrick protested. "Did you give up?"

Jack didn't answer, just backed up slowly.

"No hard feelings?" Patrick put out his hand, but Jack only backed away from the edge of the wharf. The rest of the boys scattered.

Someone cleared his throat from behind Patrick's back. Patrick turned around slowly to see the Old Man, his arms crossed, watching them a few paces away.

How much did he hear us saying? wondered Patrick.

"No hard feelings," pronounced Jack, mopping his brow with the sleeve of his shirt. "I let you win." He lowered his voice as he walked by. "But I wasn't really going to tell him."

"Uh-huh." Patrick tried to slip around the Old Man to follow Michael back toward the *Lady E*.

"Duggan?" The Old Man stopped them with a word and Jack froze.

"Think you're pretty good with that stick there?"

Patrick wasn't sure if he saw fear or a grin on the other boy's face, but Jack Duggan turned slowly around at the invitation.

"No one's ever beat me, if that's what you're asking."

"Not until now, young man. To make it fair, though, I'll use just one hand."

It really wasn't much of a contest. The silver-haired paddle-steamer captain against the strapping young wrestler. At first Jack grinned as he felt his own strength.

"You're not pulling, are you?" Jack taunted the Old Man. Patrick and Michael watched silently.

"I don't want to hurt you, lad," grunted the Old Man. He kept a straight face, but the veins on his neck were popping out. "I've done this myself a time or two—when I was your age."

Jack and the Old Man stared at each other for a full minute, pulling back and forth, while Patrick held his breath. And then, just as suddenly as Jack had pulled the other boy to his feet minutes before, the Old Man pulled back with his one arm and brought an astonished John Henry Duggan to his feet.

"There you are, lad." The Old Man chuckled and let go of the stick. "I believe that's how it's done."

"Y-yes, sir," stuttered Jack, walking slowly away.

"Oh, and Jack—"

Jack stopped but didn't turn around.

"The name you were wonderin' about."

"Sir?"

"Hughes. It's Adam Hughes. Not a big secret after all."

Patrick caught his breath. *He heard everything we said!*

CHAPTER 4

CAT IN A SACK

Patrick woke early Sunday morning, sweating and shaking. He remembered dreaming about his father hiding in a tree with the koala, then the Old Man chasing Patrick, trying to club him over the head with his charts because Patrick had sunk the paddle steamer and lied about it.

Crazy . . . Patrick tried not to think about his dream as he settled back down and listened to the early morning sounds: The musical paddling of tiny waves gathering under a corner of the paddle steamer's hull. A creaking and groaning of ropes that held them tied to the wharf. Michael's snore. Patrick dozed for what felt like only a few minutes until his mother shook him gently by the shoulder.

"Up, up, up, Patrick. We're going to be late for church."

When Patrick opened his eyes again, the morning sunlight hit him full in the face. His mother was standing in front of him, dressed in her high-collared dark green dress fringed with lace. It was frayed and probably out of fashion, but it was clean and pressed. Becky flashed around behind her in the paddle steamer's main salon, checking a mirror to fix her hair. Her plain, ankle-length blue gingham dress flapped around like a flag as she hurried to get ready.

"Come on, sleepyhead," his sister challenged him. "We tiptoed around to let you sleep an extra half hour."

Patrick groaned and rolled over on his cot, trying to think of a reason to stay under the covers.

My stomach doesn't feel too good all of a sudden, he told himself. *In fact, now that I think about it, my head hurts a bit, too. Actually, quite a bit.*

"I can't go today, Ma," he groaned, adding up his list of excuses again.

"That's not like you, Patrick." Mrs. McWaid reached down to feel his forehead. "You said you really liked the church last week. Everyone was very nice there."

"I know that, Ma. It's just that . . . please, I just don't feel very good."

His mother frowned, then looked at the brass ship's clock on the wall.

"Well, your brother and Becky and I need to get going. I'm not sure where the captain is. You stay here, then. We'll be back in a couple of hours."

Patrick sighed when they left and buried his face in his pillow. It was true about his head; it had been throbbing for the past day, especially every time he saw the Old Man. Now it seemed worse.

"You in there, boy?" came the Old Man's gravelly voice only a few minutes after the others had left.

He found out about the map! worried Patrick. *And now he's coming to get me!*

The door cracked open, and the Old Man poked his face into the salon. "Saw your ma on the wharf. Said you were still in bed or some such foolishness."

From where he peeked out from under the covers, Patrick gulped and started to sweat. *He's killed three men.* Jack's story echoed in his mind. *And now it's going to be three men and a boy.*

"I was just coming to check on you."

Patrick nodded weakly. *Why would the Old Man do that?*

"Going to church?" squeaked Patrick, trying to look as pleasant as he could.

A weak grin cracked across the man's weathered face as he stepped into the salon. "Me? No. I haven't been to church since . . ."

His voice trailed off, and the grin faded as if he had run across an unwelcome memory. "Well, I ought to go see if I can find you and your family a ride to Erin's Landing tomorrow."

The cabin at Erin's Landing. Patrick had almost forgotten about the Old Man's place, where they could stay while the Old Man was gone. The *Lady Elisabeth*, after all, was nearly loaded with supplies and wool.

"What's ailing you?" The Old Man stooped down for a closer look as Patrick remembered what Jack had said about the Old Man throwing him into the river.

"I-I'm fine!" Patrick yelped, then felt silly. Still, he held the covers tightly around his chin.

"A little work would do you good," the Old Man finally told him, holding out an ax from behind his back. "Here, I was getting tired of cutting down that wood for the boiler. You do some."

Patrick just nodded as he sat up and took the rough wooden handle.

"Get some pants on, and I'll show you what I need."

Patrick limped along behind the Old Man out to a pile of wood by the forward deck, where pieces of firewood for the steam boiler needed splitting.

"Here, see these pieces?" The Old Man pointed. "I want them all no bigger than this. Take a few minutes at it." He held out his hands to show Patrick what he meant before he left.

After the Old Man disappeared, Patrick tried a few swings, slowly at first, then with more energy. Before long he flew at the wood, swinging and chopping, forgetting the headache, forgetting the stomachache, forgetting almost everything except the ripped chart upstairs. Swing and chop. Watch the wood explode apart. Harder. Still, all he could see in his mind was the broken chart. The ax nearly sang in his hands as he swung it over his head. Faster. His heart pumped as if it would burst inside his chest. He jumped when he felt someone's hand on his shoulder.

"Whoa. You're like a wild animal, lad." The Old Man had returned.

Patrick let the Old Man take the ax and took a deep breath to stop his own trembling. "I have to show you something, sir."

He can throw me into the river, thought Patrick, *but I can't keep this secret anymore*.

Patrick didn't wait for an answer, just pulled himself up the ladder as best he could and limped into the wheelhouse.

"What are you doing?" asked the Old Man. "You've been splitting wood for only five minutes."

"I broke it," Patrick blurted out, just hoping he wouldn't start crying.

"Broke what?"

"The maps. See?" Patrick turned the crank that pulled the scrolls of maps around until he reached the part where it was torn. "I didn't mean to. I fell when I was trying to read that certificate on the wall to see what your real name was."

He acted out what had happened. "And when the chart ripped, I was afraid you would be angry, so we rolled it back up so you wouldn't see the tear right away—or at least by the time you found it, you would be far enough away so that if you were upset, you wouldn't be able to throw me in the river in a sack. . . ."

Patrick's voice trailed off, and he fiddled with the ripped chart, afraid to look up at the Old Man, who didn't say anything for a very long minute.

"How old are you, boy?"

"Twelve, sir."

"Twelve years old, and you still *believed* all that nonsense Jack Duggan probably told you about how I throw people into the river like a cat in a sack?"

Patrick shook his head. "No, sir, I didn't believe it. I mean, I'm sorry. I guess I wasn't sure."

"I think our little stick match the other day might have cured Jack's storytelling for a while. But that's not important. Anything else you need to say to me?"

Patrick thought for a moment. "No, sir, I'm just sorry I broke it and then lied trying to keep it a secret. I'm terribly sorry. It's not Jack's fault. Just mine. But you already knew all about it, didn't you?"

A grin seemed to flicker for a moment on the Old Man's wrinkled face, but he quickly turned serious. "You're not a very good liar. Stay that way. Too many liars around here already."

"I'm sorry," said Patrick for the third time.

"That's quite enough." This time the Old Man's gruff expression returned. "But that doesn't change the fact that my map is ripped."

Patrick hung his head and waited for his punishment.

"Here's what I want you to do. First, I want you to go catch up with your ma at church if it's not over. Doesn't look like you're too ill to go anymore."

"I'm feeling better now." His ankle still smarted if he turned it the wrong way, but all the rest of the aches and pains seemed to have disappeared.

"When I get back, I'll have plenty of extra chores for you." The Old Man dismissed him with a slap on his shoulder. "I expect you to repay me for this damage with your work. Now get going."

For a second Patrick thought about sliding down the ladder again, but he remembered his ankle. Except for that, he felt as if he could have floated from the *Lady Elisabeth* straight up to the wharf without touching a step.

Thank you, Lord. He couldn't hold back the silent prayer. *I'm sorry I tried to hide from the Old Man. And from you, too.*

From the bottom of the ladder next to the dock, he reached quickly down into the cool river water, washed his face, and slicked back his hair. He shook his head like a dog after a bath and smiled up at the sunshine.

"Thank you, sir!" Patrick called back as he climbed carefully up the ladder and limped as fast as he could across the wharf.

"Maybe I'll keelhaul you under the boat so you can clean the slime with a brush!" the Old Man shouted after him. It was the closest thing to a joke Patrick had ever heard from the man.

At least I hope it's a joke, thought Patrick as he hurried up High Street toward the whitewashed steeple of the little church.

His smile quickly turned to a frown, though, when he saw a

crowd of about fifteen men gathered around the front window of the newspaper office. One of them was yelling something at the others and pointing to the newspaper displayed in the window— the newspaper with his father's description.

CHAPTER 5

THE MOB

"I'm telling you, it's up to us to do something about these convicts!" The man shouted and strutted as if he were running for office. "Has the constable protected you from the bushrangers?"

"No, no . . ." The other men shook their heads and murmured.

"How about you, George?" The speaker pointed at one of the men, who was holding a rifle. "You have a wife and little girl. Living out at the edge of town like you do, you're not just going to let this convict waltz right in and—"

"No! 'Course not." The murmurs were louder this time.

"I heard the Nicholsons have lost two horses," one of the men piped up.

"There, you see?" The speechmaker slammed his fist in his palm. "First he's stealing horses, pretty soon it'll be . . ."

Patrick stood trembling, rooted in place a few steps back from the mob, listening to the pitch grow higher and higher as the man at the front whipped them up.

"Mac-weed, or Mac-wade, whatever his name is. He's the first order of business," shouted the mob leader. "Constable Fitzgerald says he's doing everything he can. Well, that's not good enough!"

Someone whooped and shot a pistol in the air, adding to the frenzy of the crowd.

"We're going to show him how Echuca men take care of their own. Get your dogs, McKenzie!"

That was all Patrick needed to hear. He looked uncertainly back toward the wharf, then up the street toward the church. Slipping away from the group, he limped as fast as his legs would move him around the crowd and up to the side entrance of the little wooden church.

I've got to tell Becky and Ma what's going on.

From inside, the pastor's bell-like voice drifted out through an open window into the still morning air.

"Blessed are you when people insult you . . . and falsely say all kinds of evil against you. . . ."

Patrick recognized the words of Jesus, from the Sermon on the Mount. It had always been one of his favorite parts of the Bible, but at that moment all he could think about were the men down the street, angrily shaking their fists at his father—a man they didn't even know.

Patrick took a deep breath, then slowly turned the doorknob and pushed open the side door. The pastor, a middle-aged man with bright eyes and a smiling face, was still reading from the Sermon on the Mount. He winked when he saw Patrick slip in quietly next to Becky.

"I thought you were sick," Becky whispered into his ear. Michael was fidgeting on the plain wooden bench next to her, beside their mother.

"Becky." Patrick tugged on his sister's hand. "I have to tell you something."

"Shh." His sister tried to pull back her hand and gave him a warning look with her eyes. But he wouldn't let go.

"It's an emergency," he whispered. "About Pa. You've got to come outside now!"

Several women in the back row stared at them as Patrick dragged his sister, brother, and mother out the side entrance.

"What's going on, Patrick?" asked Michael in his usual loud voice.

Mrs. McWaid put her hand on her youngest son's shoulder and turned to Patrick.

"All right, young man." She looked at Patrick sternly. "We leave you moaning and groaning in bed, and now you come dragging us out of church right in the middle of the sermon. What's wrong with you?"

"It's them." Patrick pointed down the street at the mob, still assembled in front of the newspaper office. "They're talking and yelling about how they're going to track down Pa."

Their mother looked down the street and bit her lip. "I saw the notice. But how do you know?"

"Ma, I'm sure. They're getting dogs and everything. The mob leader even said Pa's name. And now they think Pa's been stealing horses, so they're all upset."

Becky closed her eyes and sighed. "What are we going to do?"

Their mother opened her mouth a couple of times, but nothing came out. From the street they heard an occasional roar from the crowd, which had grown to about twenty or thirty men. From behind them, inside the church, they could still hear the pastor's clear voice.

"Ma?" Patrick asked quietly.

She finally nodded. "The captain will know what to do. Don't look at the men when we pass."

She marched them back to the wharf, looking straight ahead, while Patrick strained to catch everything the men were saying.

"I think he headed south," said one, "toward the Bendigo gold-fields."

"Ah no," argued another. "That's too far. I say he's around here."

Their mother pulled them along. "Keep walking," she whispered nervously in Patrick's ear.

One of the mob, a younger man, noticed the four of them hurrying past. "Get tired of the sermon?"

A couple of his friends laughed. Patrick stopped short, and he felt the color rise in his cheeks.

"What do *you* know about sermons?" Patrick took a step forward without thinking.

The younger man laughed and held up his fists. "Well, how about that. A fighter."

"Patrick!" Becky grabbed his arm and pulled him away from the crowd.

"Yeh, Patrick." The young man made a couple of pretend swings and turned back to his friends. "Better go home with your mum and close the doors, or this McWaid fellow might come knocking."

The others laughed again as Patrick stumbled after his sister back to the safety of the wharf.

"I'm sorry," Patrick mumbled as he helped his mother down the ladder to the *Lady Elisabeth*. "I didn't mean to . . ."

"Oh, Patrick." His mother sighed. "That temper of yours is going to get you into a lot of trouble someday."

"Someday?" added Becky. "What about already? I thought you were going to start a riot, Patrick, right there in the street."

"A riot? I wasn't going to fight anyone. He just—"

"All right," interrupted their mother. "We don't need any of that right now."

She stopped short on the deck as Constable Fitzgerald stepped out to meet them, followed by the Old Man.

"G'day, Mrs. McWaid. Children." He tipped his helmet as he ducked through the door and stepped into the sunshine.

"Hello, Constable," she replied politely.

"I was just leaving. The captain here was kind enough to show me through his vessel." He checked his pocket watch. "Aren't you back a little early from church?"

"A little," she replied. "Did you find what you were looking for?"

The tall, mustached gentleman shook his head but smiled. "I'm afraid I did not. But I shall keep looking, I assure you."

With another tip of his helmet he was up the ladder and gone. Patrick let out his breath.

"Was he . . ." started Becky, but she couldn't finish her question.

Patrick knew the constable had surely been searching for their father on the *Lady E*. Mrs. McWaid put her hand on her daughter's shoulder.

"It doesn't matter, Becky," she told her. "What's more urgent now is that there's an angry group of men to be dealt with."

Mrs. McWaid explained to the Old Man what they had seen, letting Patrick and Becky fill in the details. As they did, the Old Man's expression grew darker and darker, like a storm cloud gathering force.

"I know those men." He paced to the railing and looked out at the muddy river. "But I can't say I blame 'em, with all the bushrangers around here. Just like I can't blame Fitzgerald. He's only doing his job."

"But they said they're going to track down our pa," said Patrick. "We can't just sit here and let them. We should go out there, too."

The Old Man grabbed Patrick's shirt, not roughly, but he held on by the sleeve.

"Now, listen, boy. Those busybodies won't get far, and you're not going to go crashing out there in the bush alone."

"I didn't mean alone," Patrick protested.

From the town they could hear the baying of someone's hound dogs. The Old Man let go of Patrick's sleeve.

"Even with dogs, they won't get far." The Old Man turned back to face them. "They don't know where to look, and there's not a tracker among 'em. And neither is the constable, by the way."

They listened to the dogs for a few minutes, and a chill traveled up Patrick's spine. Finally the Old Man turned and shuffled away without another word. One by one the others followed, leaving Patrick alone on the deck, looking out over the muddy river.

The prison officials, they're probably looking for Pa. Patrick started counting on his fingers.

Then there's Constable Fitzgerald.

Two fingers.

And now the mob . . . and all their dogs. He didn't want to count anymore.

CHAPTER 6

ARRIVAL AT ERIN'S LANDING

"Boys!" Someone whistled from up on the wharf, and Patrick looked up to see the Old Man waving for them to come. "Wagon's leaving for Erin's Landing."

Patrick didn't waste any time stowing away the Monday morning breakfast dishes and grabbing up the sack of clothes the Old Man had given him.

"Is that where we're going, Patrick?" asked Michael as they climbed the ladder back up to the wharf. "Erin's Landing?"

"That's what the Old Man calls his place. Hang on to your animal."

"Ow!" Michael lifted one of the koala's paws from his shoulder. "He's holding on to me."

"Well, look at that," said a little man up on the wharf. He was standing next to his open wagon, straightening the reins of his horses, two poor sway-backed creatures who looked very ready for retirement. "Don't believe I've seen one of those koalas so close up before."

The man, who wore a full black beard and a thin, frayed shirt, spoke with an accent Patrick had never heard before. The Old Man introduced him as Claude Duggan, a French-Englishman who had come to Australia with his family a few years back. The smiling, dark-haired Mr. Duggan helped Becky and Mrs. McWaid into the wagon while Patrick and Michael piled into the back with their collection of bags.

Mrs. McWaid gave her son a concerned look. "Patrick, are you still limping?"

Patrick shook his head. "All better, Ma. Well, almost. Not to worry."

The Old Man winked at their mother as he hoisted another box of groceries into the back of the wagon.

"He'll be all right, Mrs. McWaid. Just needs to take care when he's jumping down from high places."

Mrs. McWaid frowned and shook her head.

"And what's all this, Old Man?" asked Mr. Duggan.

"Enough basics to keep them going for a while, Claude. Flour, salt pork, dried beans. But I want you and the boy to check on them in a few days."

The boy? wondered Patrick, and then he remembered with a quiet groan. *This man has to be related to John Henry Duggan.*

"You're very kind, Captain." Patrick's mother held out her hand. "I can't thank you enough for what you've done already."

"You won't be thanking him so much once you've seen the humpy," laughed Mr. Duggan. "We call it 'Erin's Wreck.' "

"You're very funny, Claude," replied the Old Man. "But don't forget, I built the place myself."

"Ah yes, Erin's *Landing*. Sounds very elegant. Like a fine restaurant in Paris."

"You wouldn't understand."

"Try me."

The Old Man sighed. "We Irish get the name *Erin* from *Eire*, the wife of MacColl, one of the early Irish kings." He sounded almost like a schoolteacher. "I just thought it was a fitting name for my little homestead, too."

"*Eire*-land. Ah yes." Mr. Duggan winked at them. "He's an Irish history expert, too, but a housekeeper he's not."

"Didn't I tell them it needs a woman's touch?" The Old Man gave Mr. Duggan an exasperated slap on the leg with the back of his hand.

"Woman's touch, ha!" The Frenchman responded good-naturedly. "If that was all Erin's Landing needed, I'd live there myself."

"Except for the fact that no one invited you," replied the Old Man. Patrick got the impression that the two men enjoyed their friendly argument.

"I might as well; you're never there." The man whistled as he gave the reins a shake, then looked around. "Where's Jack? Jack!"

Jack Duggan came trotting down the street behind them as they rumbled slowly along. He jumped and hauled himself into the back of the wagon.

"It's you!" cried Michael.

Jack held up his hands and nodded toward the driver. "Who else? He's my father. I hear we're going to be neighbors."

"Mrs. McWaid." The Old Man nodded politely as Claude Duggan's horses eagerly pulled them away from the wharf, then through the town. Even though it had been hours since the mob had met in the street the day before, Patrick was still relieved not to see anyone in front of the newspaper office.

"I thought you lived here in town," Patrick told Jack, who had settled in on top of the luggage. The older boy shook his head.

"Who told you that? We live just outside of town, but we come in all the time 'cause my father works in the boatyards. I come with him to help out most of the time."

"Hmm." Patrick nodded.

"Ma, what's a humpy?" asked Michael, holding on to the side of the wagon to keep from being bumped out.

"Where did you hear that, dear?"

"That's where he said we're going." Michael looked at the driver. "To the Old Man's humpy."

"A shack, a cabin." Mr. Duggan smiled at them over his shoulder. He barely paid attention to the road, but the horses seemed to know the way. "Here in Australia, we have new words for things. I think it's maybe the work of the English—they come over, and maybe they don't want to be English anymore. They want to be Australians now. So they invent new words."

Mrs. McWaid laughed. "You would think they could come up with better-sounding words than ones like humpy, though."

Mr. Duggan shrugged. "After fifteen years I'm still learning how to speak like the Australians. My wife, she's English, so it's not so hard for her and the children. You'll learn, too."

Patrick nodded and tried to shade his head as they bounced along. A pack of five or six stray dogs followed them to the edge of town, sniffing hungrily. Patrick couldn't help thinking about his father and the dogs that were probably after him.

Lord, please don't let those dogs . . . He couldn't finish his prayer, just hoped God knew what he meant.

"Hey, you falling asleep already?" Jack kicked Patrick's foot.

Patrick shook his head and sat up straighter. "I'm awake. How come we're not following the river?"

"Quicker this way." Jack waved his hand like a snake. "River goes like this, but we just cut across. See?"

Patrick nodded. Beyond the town they headed across gray river flats, the horses' hooves kicking up tiny clouds of dust, until they found themselves in a tangle of blue-gray gum trees, the kind with the pale white bark that seemed to weep in strips to the forest floor. Patrick liked the smell, something like a light, sweet candy.

"Look over there!" Michael pointed ahead of them. "Parrots!"

Patrick looked to see hundreds of white birds lift into the air in a beautiful, shrieking cloud.

"Cockatoos," Mr. Duggan corrected him. "When they fly like that, it means more rain."

"Honest?" Michael practically stood up for a better look, and the man nodded while he put out his hand for Michael to sit down.

"That, or a couple of bushrangers just scared them out of their tree. Like those kangaroos over there." He pointed at a family of four or five gray bouncing shapes disappearing into the bush.

"They're beautiful." Mrs. McWaid clapped her hands.

"What's a bushranger?" asked Michael.

Mr. Duggan laughed as they bounced along the rutted road. "An Australian outlaw." He held up a finger in a pretend pistol. "I hear there's a gang somewhere around here."

"Around here?" Michael's eyes grew wide at the story, and he looked around.

"Ha," replied Mr. Duggan. "Don't you worry about them. They're not going to bother a kid like you."

Mrs. McWaid gave Michael a smile as if to say, "He's telling you the truth."

I hope he's right, Patrick thought to himself.

Mr. Duggan continued for the next half hour with his stories of how he and his family had come to Australia from England, about how they had lived in France before that, about their daughter, who would enjoy meeting Becky, and about the last time the river had flooded.

"Which way is the river?" asked Becky, craning her neck.

Mr. Duggan pointed to a line of trees on their right. "Over there is your Erin's Landing Estate."

"And your family?" Becky wanted to know. "Where do you live?"

"Almost within cooee," he replied, and Mrs. McWaid laughed.

"You'll have to explain *that* one," she told him.

Mr. Duggan replied by cupping a hand to his mouth, taking a deep breath, and hollering "COO-EEE!"

Becky put her hands to her ears and giggled.

"That's what my Australian children taught me," explained Mr. Duggan with a satisfied smile. "If you can hear the aborigine cooee yell, I suppose you're next-door neighbors. But you can't, so we're *almost* next-door neighbors. We'll come sometime to visit—my wife and Dominique, too. They'd like to see your koala. And you need anything, well, you let us know."

"We'll just cooee," said Michael, but his mother stopped him before he could try it out.

"Later, Michael."

Soon they could see the humpy—the cabin—set among the trees inside a bend in the Murray River.

"This is Erin's Landing?" asked Becky.

Mr. Duggan nodded.

Patrick slipped off the side of the wagon and sprinted ahead. "I'm going to be the first one there!" he called back. Suddenly he felt a little silly, but still he kept running until he reached the house.

"Where's the front door?" he called back, then ran around the side. The small house certainly wasn't built by anyone who had been overly concerned about making it square. As far as Patrick could tell, it had been pieced together from parts of three or four different riverboats. Nameplates from at least two, the *Nellie* and the *Invincible*, hung at crazy angles from the outside walls.

"Maybe there isn't a front door," Patrick mumbled to himself, but finally around to the side he found a small veranda, or porch, and a door swinging open to the breeze.

The windows were small and round, like a ship's, and a stubby mast with a tattered blue triangle pennant crowned the knit-together collection of ship pieces. Overlooking the river, the salvaged wheelhouse of a paddle steamer offered a view through the trees.

"It's a ship!" cried Michael as the wagon jerked to a stop. "Isn't it?"

Mr. Duggan laughed as he hopped down from his seat. "I'm not sure what it is, either. The Old Man's grand estate. He had pieces of dead riverboats hauled up here to this high spot, and then he leaves it all for the animals to live in. And now you."

"I think it's a crazy place," commented Jack, not getting out of the wagon.

Becky climbed down from her perch on the wagon. "It looks as if the place is held together with flowers." She reached out to pick one of the bright purple blooms from the vines that seemed to weave themselves across the wall, in and out of the shingles, and she inhaled the sweet scent. Their mother, though, could only stand by the flowers, tears running down her cheeks.

"What's wrong, Ma?" asked Patrick. "Don't you like the flowers?"

Mrs. McWaid didn't answer right away, as if she were far away. "Ma?" probed Michael. "Are you all right?"

Their mother slowly nodded and reached out to pick one of the flowers. "Your father always promised me that someday he would buy me a house in the country with a flower garden." She smiled and wiped the tears from her eyes, and Becky put her arm around her mother.

"We'll find him, Ma," she told her.

"I can smell them from here," said Mrs. McWaid, closing her eyes and smiling.

A fluttering of wings flashed out through the open front door, nearly knocking them over. Michael jumped and giggled at the same time.

"What was that?" asked Mrs. McWaid, grabbing Michael by the shoulders.

"Bronze-winged pigeons," explained Mr. Duggan, coming up from behind. "Makes a good dinner, if you can catch one."

Minutes later Michael had discovered the pigeon's roost, the lizards, and the family of possums that had taken up homes in the Old Man's riverboat-on-land.

"Can we keep them?" whined Michael.

"Out!" ordered their mother. "I don't care how many animals you have, but they all have to live outside."

"This is great!" said Patrick from the wheelhouse. "We can see when the Old Man is coming back down the river from here."

Mrs. McWaid looked up into the rafters and sighed. "Spiders, birds, little creatures . . . I'm thankful for the roof over our heads, but I'm going to need everyone's help to sweep and wash this place before we can even sleep here."

"And all these animal nests have to go, too," added Becky, poking at a pile of sticks in the corner with her foot. Suddenly she screamed, and Patrick saw the dark flash of a large snake attach itself to his sister's ankle.

CHAPTER 7

TIGER SNAKE

"Ma!" cried Becky, and she did a desperate dance across the bare wood floor, the snake still attached. It was at least six feet long, almost black, and squirming wildly.

Mrs. McWaid froze for just an instant, about as long as Patrick did, as the snake swung around and swatted them both in the leg with its tail.

"Becky!" screamed their mother, throwing up her hands as if they were in a holdup. "Stand still!"

Patrick didn't have time to think as he stood rooted next to an old wooden chair. In the next moment he lifted the chair up over his head, then brought it down on the writhing animal again and again until he was holding nothing but splinters and the snake had stopped moving. Becky was on her knees on the floor, sobbing, while their mother tried to grab the lifeless snake.

"Don't touch it!" commanded Mr. Duggan, bursting in through the open door. "It's a tiger snake."

"But it's dead," protested Mrs. McWaid. "Patrick broke its back."

Jack came running in from the outside and skidded to a stop when he saw the snake. "What's going on?"

His father didn't answer but quickly checked the nest in the corner of the room for more snakes while Patrick took one of the broken chair legs and lifted the dead snake off the floor.

"Got it," Jack reported when his father kicked the snake toward the door.

"Where did it bite you?" asked Mr. Duggan, but Becky was too upset to answer. Mrs. McWaid pulled off her high ankle boot for a closer look while they laid Becky out on a dusty cot.

"I'm not sure," Becky finally squeaked, lying on her back. Her face was as pale as the ashes in the fireplace next to the cot.

"The bite will be small," said Mr. Duggan. "But we should be able to see it."

"I'm not sure if it actually bit her," Patrick announced.

"What do you mean?" asked Mrs. McWaid, on her knees next to Becky.

"The snake . . ." Patrick was still shaking. "The snake looked like it was caught on her bootlaces, as if it bit but didn't get through the boot."

"I don't see any bites." Michael came up to look.

"It happened so f-fast," gasped Becky. "It just snapped up at me like a spring, and then . . . then it leadn't woot, it w-wouldn't . . ."

"That's all right, Becky." Mrs. McWaid ran her fingers across her daughter's cheek. "You're going to be all right."

"It wouldn't let go." Becky wiped the tears from her eyes when she finally got the words out.

"You were very fortunate," said Mr. Duggan, holding up her boot. He pointed at a small, needle-like fang that hung in the laces like a fishhook. "Looks like you're right, Patrick. These snakes don't usually hang on. But see how close it came."

"Is that a tooth?" Michael tried to inspect his sister's shoe, but Mr. Duggan held him at arm's length.

"A tiger snake is more poisonous than a cobra. A small person like your sister might live five minutes after a bite."

Still kneeling at her daughter's side, Mrs. McWaid let go of her tears in a prayer. Patrick couldn't understand all the words, but he knew exactly what his mother was praying. She thanked God for bringing them to the Old Man's place, for protecting Becky, even for helping them find their father—which of course hadn't happened yet.

Thank you was all Patrick could manage. The rest stuck in his throat, and he didn't want to cry in front of strangers, especially not Jack. When Patrick opened his eyes, his mother was helping Becky sit up, and Mr. Duggan was making the sign of the cross on his forehead and chest. Jack stood by the door and scratched his head.

"Ah-men," said Mr. Duggan, and he gripped Patrick's shoulder. "That was quick thinking, young man. That snake could have bitten through your sister's boot, but you—"

"You smashed him before he got a chance," finished Michael, looking in a kind of horrified fascination at what was left of the reptile.

"Yeh, pretty impressive job with the chair." Jack seemed to look at Patrick with a new respect.

"Ma, do you think we can hang him up on the wall as a souvenir?" asked Michael.

Jack laughed.

"Ohh," groaned their mother in disapproval.

Mr. Duggan picked up the snake with a piece of the chair and headed out the door.

"How about just the skin?" Michael wouldn't give up. "I can skin him, and then we can stretch the skin out like—"

"I'll take care of this animal, Mrs. McWaid," Mr. Duggan told them over his shoulder.

"You mean the snake," asked Patrick, "or the little boy?"

Mrs. McWaid smiled weakly, obviously not yet ready for a joke. "Are there any other poisonous beasts hiding around here?"

"No need to worry much about snakes," Mr. Duggan told their mother. "We really don't see them too often."

Becky smiled for the first time and gave Patrick a kiss on the cheek after she stood up. "Thanks, little brother. Now I know why the Old Man said his place could use a woman's touch."

"Becky," protested their mother, "you should rest awhile longer."

Becky dusted herself off and looked back at the bed. "It's a bit dirty, Ma. Besides, I think I'd like to make sure there aren't any more snakes around."

She found a ragged broom leaning against the wall by the door and went right to work kicking up dust. She approached each corner cautiously, the broom out in front, poking into the darkness.

Mrs. McWaid dried her tears with a corner of the sleeve on her dress. "You children just be careful of any other wild animals, do you hear?"

"We'll be careful, Ma," answered Michael, looking out the door. "But I still wish we could save the snakeskin."

Becky gave Michael a swat with her broom. "No more about that. Promise?"

Michael yelped, and Patrick began gathering up the pieces of splintered wood.

"Do you think the Old Man is going to be upset about his chair?" he asked Becky, thinking again about the ripped charts in the *Lady Elisabeth*. When the rest of them laughed at the question, Patrick smiled, too, but he hadn't meant it as a joke.

"We'll be getting along, Mrs. McWaid," called Mr. Duggan, pulling his old horses around by the front door while Jack climbed back up into the wagon. "It's a bit of a walk, but you can send someone by our house if you need anything. And I'll have Jack check on you once in a while."

"Thank you so much for all your help, Mr. Duggan." Their mother stood in the doorway. "Jack, too. I'm sorry for all the trouble."

The man grinned and waved off a fly as he stepped up to the wagon's seat. "I can see that it's going to take a lot more than a little snake to chase you away from here." He pointed at Becky. "I'll bring my girl by sometime. You and Dominique are about the same age."

Becky smiled back. "I'd like that, Mr. Duggan."

"Oh, and I'm heading back to town in a few days; the boatyard has some more work for me. We'll stop by on the way just in case you need anything."

"You're very kind, Mr. Duggan," said their mother.

Mr. Duggan smiled and nodded, and Patrick listened to Jack's *ha-ha-ha* bird call as they watched the Duggans' wagon disappear down the lane.

Michael ran out to climb one of the smaller scrub pines. "First thing we need to do is build Christopher a tree house," he shouted down.

"Wait a minute, young man," their mother warned him. "First we have to clean up the house we're going to live in before we go building koala houses."

"But, Ma . . ."

Their mother shook her head. "But nothing. Becky and I will sweep out the inside if you boys will haul out the birds' nests and . . ."

It was grimy, dusty work, but Patrick didn't mind. They spent the rest of the day sweeping, scrubbing, pounding out rugs, chasing out spiders from the rafters, and patching holes in the roof. It was late afternoon when Patrick and Michael at last had a moment to rest down by the river.

"I like this river," announced Michael, scooping a clean bucketful of water. The bucket was full of holes, and they watched it drain onto the muddy bank. "Reminds me of the River Liffey, back home in Dublin. Do you miss Dublin, Patrick?"

Patrick swatted at a mosquito and crouched by the water's edge. "I miss walking down the streets," he finally admitted. "Talking to all the street sellers. And I miss our neighborhood. The organ grinder with the monkey."

Michael grinned, remembering.

"But I like this place," Patrick went on. "It's different. I like the sun."

Michael looked up at the sun and sneezed. "I guess I do, too. I'd like it more if Pa were here."

Patrick didn't answer, so Michael grabbed a rope that was hanging above their heads. "Look, Patrick! I can swing all the way out over the river without getting wet."

The Old Man had set up a kind of homemade crane on the

riverbank, obviously used to haul things out of boats. Hanging on to the crane's hook, Michael swung in a loop out over the river, skimming the water with his feet.

"Don't do that, Michael!"

"You're always telling me not to do things, Patrick. I'm careful."

"Sure you are, but I don't want you to get hurt or fall in the water." He stood up and tried to haul his little brother back, but Michael had already returned to dry land. "Don't swing out like that again."

"But it's fun, Patrick. You don't have to get so upset. Why don't you try it?"

Patrick squeezed his fists hard to keep his brother from seeing that he was shaking. It wasn't as bad as it used to be, but he could still imagine when his youngest brother, Sean, was still alive, playing on the bridge back home in Dublin before he fell into the river—and drowned.

"All right," Michael finally told him. He clutched the rope and pushed back and forth from the shore. "I'll go again if you don't want to. One, two . . ."

"Don't, Sean!" Patrick grabbed Michael by the arm. "You can't . . ."

Michael stared up at his brother with wide eyes and wrinkled his forehead. "Why did you call me Sean?"

Patrick closed his eyes, shook his head, and sighed. "I'm sorry, Michael. I just can't help remembering. Look, let's go up and check on your koala. Maybe I'll help you build that tree fort you were talking about."

"No kidding?"

"Sure." Patrick shrugged his shoulders and followed Michael up the bank.

"Coo-EEE, Christopher!" yelled Michael, sprinting up the path. "Guess what we're going to build for you!"

CHAPTER 8

WHERE'S MICHAEL?

For the next three nights their mother slept on the only bed in the house, while Becky, Michael, and Patrick swung on hammocks they had made out of poles, blankets, and rope. Patrick was especially proud of his ropework, even though he had to admit the hammocks weren't exactly comfortable. His back made a cracking noise as he tried to straighten out early Thursday morning, and he rolled out of the hammock to escape into the soft morning air.

The river's a good morning place, he thought, making tracks with his bare feet through the dewy grass around the cabin. The sandy earth felt cool between his toes, and as he stepped toward the river he dug them in deeper to feel the coolness. Slipping the final few feet down the bank, he found a place on a big, exposed root of a coolibah tree to watch the silent, glassy surface of the river.

The Old Man's loading crane, the one Michael had been playing on a few days before, was around a little bend, just out of sight upriver. By Patrick's tree root the water seemed somehow more still. Here and there ripples broke the surface, but the brown tea water just flowed by. He didn't even want to throw a rock, afraid it would break the perfect stillness or ruin the reflections of the golden-leaved trees draped around the edges like old friends.

"It's pretty here," he whispered, listening for the sounds of the birds and breathing deeply the damp, full flavor of the river. The Old Man had said something once about being able to navigate up and down the river just using his nose, and Patrick thought maybe he knew what he meant. Here he couldn't quite throw a rock to the opposite bank, and the water smelled deep and powerful.

Something hooted from the top of his tree, almost directly above. Patrick jumped, but then smiled. *Just an owl.*

In the distance he heard something else, this time not an owl or a river sound, but the unmistakable baying of a pack of hounds. The barking grew louder, and Patrick closed his eyes.

I shouldn't be sitting here, he told himself. *I should be out trying to find Pa like they are.*

The baying sound drew even closer, and there was a rustling behind him.

"Hear that?" asked Becky. She was standing on the top of the bank, ten feet above.

Patrick looked up at her and nodded. "They've been out in the woods for the past few minutes."

"What are you doing down here?"

"Just sitting. Watching the river. Trying to figure out how we could ever find Pa."

Becky sighed and put her hands on her hips, looking around. The sound of the hounds was getting closer, and it made Patrick wonder what kind of scent they were following.

"I wonder where they're going," said Becky.

Patrick picked up a stick and made a couple of lines in the smooth, gray river dirt. "I saw the Old Man's charts. If this is the Murray River, then the Campaspe River empties into it right here, where the waters meet in Echuca."

"What are you trying to say?" Becky walked around to orient herself with Patrick's drawing. The hounds passed by on the other side of the river, louder than ever.

"I'm trying to say that if Pa is around here somewhere, don't you think he would stick close to the rivers?"

Becky shook her head. "I don't know. That's what Jefferson thought. And that's where all the people are. I think he would try to stay where there aren't so many people."

"But he needs water. Here's what I'd do if I were a runaway prisoner." Patrick scratched out several lines running into his river map. "I'd find one of these little creeks." He pointed to the lines. "I'd sit it out for a while, and then I'd slip into Echuca to find out about our grandfather, same way we're trying to do."

"And what about when he discovers that his father isn't here?"

Patrick couldn't answer.

"All we know is that our grandfather might have lived here a long time ago," Becky continued. "No one has heard from him in years, remember?"

Patrick made a big X in the dirt and crossed his arms. "I remember, but we can't just stay here while those men with the dogs are out hunting Pa down."

They stood for a couple of minutes, staring at the water flowing past, listening to a light breeze ruffle the leaves of the trees.

"So how are we going to find him?" Becky finally asked, but Patrick had no answer.

Their mother shouted from the shack's little veranda. "Patrick! Becky! Michael! Come up for some breakfast!"

They wasted no time scrambling back to the cabin, and Patrick used his nose to follow the smell of cooking sausages.

"Wash up in that bucket," directed Mrs. McWaid after they burst in. "Especially if you've been playing with Michael's animal."

Patrick looked around the room. His mother had set tin plates out on a board they had propped up to use as a table, and she was now standing watch over a small fire in the river-rock fireplace.

"Where's Michael?" asked Patrick.

Mrs. McWaid frowned. "I thought he was with you, Patrick."

Patrick shook his head. "I haven't seen him since I got out of bed an hour ago. He was still sleeping."

"Well, for goodness sake." Their mother pulled her frying pan back out of the flames as the grease caught fire.

"He's probably right outside." Becky dried her hands and leaned out the front door. "Hey, Michael! Time to eat."

Patrick joined his sister at the door. "Break-fast!"

They waited, but Michael didn't answer.

"Michael?" Patrick tried once again, and Mrs. McWaid sighed.

"You children have to promise me not to go running off like that. Patrick, would you please go out and find him? Only this time, please put on some shoes. You remember what happened to—"

"I will, Ma." Patrick glanced down at his sandy feet, then found his shoes before he ran outside.

"Hey, Michael!" he yelled over and over. After a few minutes he started to run, still with his shoes in his hand. Behind him, he could hear Becky shouting Michael's name, too. In the stand of Murray pines where they had started to build a tree house and a cage for the koala, nothing. Down the road that led through the woods to the cabin, nothing. Finally, he checked by the river, the place where Michael had played on the Old Man's crane.

"What if . . . ?" He pulled at the handle of the crane, which had been left in position over the water. "Michael!"

He started shouting again, louder and louder, then ran along the river for a few yards to get a better view downstream.

"Michael!" He yelled himself hoarse.

Not again, Michael! he thought, scrambling farther down the shore. *We already went through this*. It had been only a few weeks, and Patrick could still feel the panic that had gripped him the first time he realized Michael had fallen into the Murray River. But that had been at night, and it was because of a riverboat accident. It hadn't been Michael's fault the first time. Now . . .

Something hit him on the head—it felt like an acorn—and he looked up.

"Michael! What are you doing up there? Why didn't you answer me?"

Michael was perched in the fork of a young red gum tree, clutching his bear. "I was waiting for you to find me, Patrick."

Patrick sighed and shook his head. "Well, get down out of there right now. Ma is worried about you."

"She is?" Michael slid down the trunk of the tree feet first after handing down his pet koala to Patrick. "All I did was come to look for you, and when he heard the dogs, Christopher got away from me and climbed up this tree, and I—"

"And you couldn't just leave him there," Patrick finished his brother's sentence.

"Really!" insisted Michael. "The dogs sounded like they were after a fox or something."

"Hmm."

"Didn't you hear them, Patrick?"

"I heard them. Now hurry up. Ma's making sausages for breakfast."

"Sausages!" Michael galloped up the hill to the cabin with his koala riding on his shoulders, and Patrick tried to keep pace. He caught up by the veranda, where the door was open wide. The Duggans' wagon was hitched up to a tree in front, and from inside they could hear laughing.

"Jack usually comes along to help me at the boatyard," said Mr. Duggan, who was standing by the door.

Jack looked around when Patrick stepped up. "G'day, Patrick." He smiled and put out his hand.

"You're back!" Patrick returned the smile. *If we're going to be neighbors*, he thought, *maybe I can get used to Jack.*

"We told you we'd come by again in a few days, didn't we?"

"Well, yes."

"So a fellow came by the house last night," explained Mr. Duggan, "told me they were laying the keel for a new paddle steamer, might need my help this morning. Thought if your mother could spare you, you might like to ride in with us."

"Well . . ." Patrick wasn't sure.

"Your ma already said it was all right with her if you wanted to." Jack was convincing when he wanted to be. "We won't be gone all day."

As she came outside, Patrick looked at his mother for her final permission. With a smile she handed him a small bundle wrapped in a towel. "Mr. Duggan said you'd be back in just a few hours," she told him. "Here's your breakfast."

"Thanks." Patrick took his bundle and climbed up to the seat between Mr. Duggan and Jack as they started down the lane. "Bye, Ma!"

"Hey, that smells pretty good." Jack sniffed at Patrick's package.

"Jack!" Mr. Duggan scolded his son. "We've already had our breakfast."

"Maybe so, but not johnnycakes and sausages."

Patrick unwrapped the towel his mother had wrapped around three pan-fried puffy pancakes, each one stuffed with thick, juicy sausages. Patrick downed two in just a few bites, then looked at his new friends.

"Want one?" He held it out to Jack. "What did you call it?"

"Johnnycakes, and I was just kidding you. You eat it."

"No, you. My ma's a good cook."

Jack finished off the last johnnycake without any trouble as they rolled through the eucalyptus stands toward Echuca. This time the ride didn't seem as long.

"No parrots this time," said Patrick as they neared a few bark shacks on the outskirts of town.

"Cockatoos." Jack nudged Patrick in the side. "No escaped convict, either. Pa, you think he's around here somewhere?"

Mr. Duggan blew out his breath. "I think it's a bunch of foolishness, son. People getting excited over nothing. Else, we wouldn't leave your mother and Dominique alone, now, would we?"

"I suppose not."

"See? Now, I'll meet you and Patrick right back here in front of the post office at noon. You stay out of trouble, and I don't want to hear anything about you and your friends jumping uninvited on any paddle steamers, hear?"

Jack nodded seriously. He was almost bigger and stronger-looking than his father, but when Mr. Duggan talked, there was no question who was in charge.

"Come on, Patrick," said Jack, jumping down to the dirt street. "I don't have to work with my father this time, and I've got a penny. We can split some lolly."

"Great." Patrick followed Jack into a crooked wooden building topped by a large sign: *Mullarky, General Merchant*. Around the side was another entrance with yet another sign: *Mullarky, Ship Chandler*.

"More sign than shop here, eh?" Patrick said aloud as they stepped inside.

"Shh!" Jack warned him. "Don't let Mr. Mullarky hear you say anything like that!"

They stepped into a dim, musty world of coiled ropes, barrels full of nails, and walls lined with everything from huge two-man saws to hammers and axes and oil lanterns. It smelled of leather gloves and fresh cans of linseed oil, and for a moment Patrick stopped to take it all in. Mullarky's store was covered from ceiling to floor with just about everything Patrick could imagine anyone might buy.

"It's bigger inside than I thought," Patrick admitted, and he followed Jack to a counter with two glass jars full of yellow and red hard candies, what Jack had called "lolly."

Jack stopped in front of one of the jars and fingered the penny in his hand. "How many for a penny, Mr. Mullarky?" Jack studied his choices while Patrick wandered around the store.

Patrick stiffened behind a display of shovels when he caught a word of what a couple of men were saying by the front door.

"Bet he won't be hard to find now," whistled a stooped, bearded old man through what remained of his teeth. "Curly red hair, dirty-looking fella, like the poster said."

"You saw him?" asked the other man. Patrick picked up a ball of twine, and his ears burned.

"Nah, but I think Nicholson did. They're going out again with the dogs."

Jack strolled over and tossed Patrick a yellow candy; Patrick missed it and it rolled into a crack in the wooden floor.

"Aw, Patrick."

"Sorry." Patrick got down on his knees and fished the candy out of the dust, trying not to miss anything the men by the door were saying.

Jack snatched the dusty candy out of his hand and popped it in his own mouth. "Here, have another one." He shoved a handful of candies in Patrick's direction while the first man continued.

"You see that fellow over there across the street, coming this way?"

The other murmured something Patrick couldn't make out.

"That Irish dandy in a bowler hat? I heard he's either a newspaper reporter or a government man, one or the other. Been asking all kinds of questions. One of those kind."

"You all right, Patrick?" asked Jack. "You look like you just died."

Patrick could only nod as they made their way to the door.

"I'm fine," he managed to croak, and he tripped out the door behind Jack. *A dirty-looking fella*, the man had said. *Curly red hair*. Patrick trembled. *Pa! It had to be. And so close . . .*

"Were they talking about the escaped prisoner in there?" Jack threw one of his candies high into the air and caught it in his mouth. "Sounds like you got in on the latest gossip."

Patrick looked across the muddy street at the newspaper office, where he knew the description of his father would still be posted. But his knees locked when he saw the man in the rounded black bowler hat staring at the notice. *Conrad Burke!* The man responsible for putting his father in prison!

"It's him," Patrick whispered.

"It's who?" Jack glanced around, scratching his head with his free hand.

Across the street the man in the round bowler pulled out a notebook from his back pocket, jotted something down, and wheeled around to cross in their direction.

"Stand right where you are," hissed Patrick, bending down and using Jack as a shield. The other boy tried to turn and look, but Patrick wouldn't let him.

"Don't move!" Patrick commanded him, and for some reason Jack listened.

The man gingerly stepped between puddles, making his way to the boards on their side.

"Is he coming this way?" Patrick was afraid to look, afraid to have Jack look.

"If you mean the man in the bowler hat, I think so. Why don't we just turn around and walk away?"

Patrick would have done that if he could have made his legs obey. An older woman looked at them curiously.

"You'd better tell me what we're doing," said Jack as they finally slipped back into Mullarky's store.

"Back so soon?" The man behind the counter looked over his glasses. The three old men had left, but with one glance out the small window beside the door, Patrick knew who was entering.

"Jack, hide me!"

This time Jack was quick on his feet. He pushed Patrick down behind the door and positioned himself where Burke would see him when he first stepped inside. Patrick crouched silently, his heart pounding, and then the door opened in his face.

"Well, hello there!" cried Jack, his face lighting up as if he were meeting an old friend. He took a few steps toward the startled man, grabbed his hand, and started pumping it. "I am so glad to see you after all this time!"

"Do I know you?" The man sounded more than confused, and still Patrick had seen only the back of his head, but Patrick knew exactly who was standing in the store. He saw Jack's eyes flicker, a signal for Patrick to escape.

"No, sir, you don't, but . . ." Jack sounded confident, but Patrick knew they were almost out of time. As quickly and as quietly as he could, he tiptoed around the door, slipped outside, and ran.

"Whoa!" cried a woman, her arms full of packages. Patrick weaved to the side, and then he felt a burning pain tear through his ankle.

"Ow!" he groaned, but he couldn't stop. He limped to the first corner and slipped around the edge of the Duke of Edinburgh Hotel, catching his breath.

Two minutes later Jack came flying by.

"There you are." Jack almost skidded off the slick boardwalk into a gutter as he raced to where Patrick was leaning against the brick wall. "That man thought I was crazy."

"He was right." Patrick smiled and shook his head. "But thanks."

"You're welcome. And now you're going to have to tell me what we just did. Who was that?"

Patrick nodded. "His name is Conrad Burke. My pa used to work for him back in Dublin."

"He came all this way, too? Why didn't you want to run into him?"

Patrick closed his eyes, trying to sort through how much he wanted to tell.

"After that act, Patrick, I have a right to know."

"I guess you do. But first let me tell you who my father is. You know that notice of the escaped convict in the newspaper office window?"

Jack hung on to every word of Patrick's story as they hurried down the street. Actually, Jack walked and Patrick limped. Patrick kept an eye out behind them, fearing Burke would show up again.

Halfway across Conolly Street they sidestepped a big red Cobb & Company stagecoach filled with people, heading for the center of town. Patrick thought he felt the ground shake under the hooves of the six grand-looking white horses pulling the stage, and he would have stood there staring, but Jack poked him in the side.

"Let me see if I understand this right." Jack pointed his finger down the street. "You say that man claims he's working for an Irish newspaper, and he's here to do a story on the colony. How do you know that?"

"That's what he told Jefferson and me on the trip up the river."

"All right. But he's *actually* been sent here by a crooked police inspector to make sure your pa doesn't tell anybody what he found out about Dublin's chief police inspector."

Patrick nodded. "I know it sounds confusing, but—"

"And if people found out the truth, the police inspector would have been in big trouble, or . . ."

"More than that. He would have gone to jail, but they put my pa in jail instead."

"There's only one thing to do, you know." Jack crossed his arms.

"We need to go out and find your pa before they do."

Patrick groaned. "I know, Jack. Don't you think I've wanted to do that?"

"But you haven't, even with that letter of yours to prove he's been here. And I'm sure Burke is the one who told the police to search the *Lady E*."

"I hadn't thought of that."

Jack pointed his thumb at his chest. "That's why you need me."

"So where do you propose we start looking?" Patrick checked down the street once more.

"We'll think of something." Jack checked to see what Patrick was looking at. "But right now we'd better take you somewhere safe for the rest of the morning before you bump into that fellow Burke again."

"You know of someplace?"

"Do I know of someplace? This is my town."

Jack checked both ways down the street, then waved Patrick down to the wharf.

"Why didn't you tell me all this before?" Jack asked as they crossed the wharf.

"Too long of a story. And besides, I didn't know who you were."

They wove their way through dock workers pushing carts around the wharf. Some waved at Jack, and the two boys continued to the end where a sad-looking barge lay rotting in the mud, half-covered in canvas tarps.

"That's it," Jack announced proudly.

"That's what?" Patrick wasn't so sure. It looked as if it had been abandoned many years ago, and he wasn't at all convinced it was floating on anything except a mud bank.

"My mates and I call it *The Pride of the Murray*." Jack waved his hand at the old barge. "The fellow in the bowler will never find you here."

"Uh . . ." Patrick looked around the wharf, hoping to find a way out. A familiar-looking wagon had pulled in from the street, and the driver was talking to one of the workers.

"Look, Jack, it's your pa."

Jack turned around to see. "I wonder what he's doing here. He's not supposed to be done for another couple of hours."

Mr. Duggan noticed them standing on the end of the wharf, whistled, and waved for them to join him. Patrick was happy to limp over to the wagon.

"There you are, boys. I thought I'd find you here."

Jack looked confused. "Weren't you supposed to be working this morning?"

"They say they're ready for me to help, and then they're not ready after all." Mr. Duggan explained with his hands as he always did. "So it's back and forth—maybe tomorrow. We'll just pick up some supplies and head home again, if it's all right with Patrick."

Patrick wasted no time stepping up into the wagon. "Fine with me."

He wasn't sure what he would do, though, if they ran into Conrad Burke on the way out of town. *Maybe I'll just hide in the back of the wagon*, he thought as Mr. Duggan and Jack loaded up a couple of sacks of flour. He scanned the people coming in and out of stores, but no Burke.

"Expecting to meet someone?" Mr. Duggan asked as he climbed back into the wagon.

"Uh . . ." Patrick stammered, not sure how much he should say. "Not expecting, exactly."

Jack's father didn't press the matter. He gave the reins a shake and pulled his old horses into a steady walk out of town.

"Hey, your ma will be surprised to see us back again so early," said Jack.

Patrick nodded and kept low, not breathing any more easily until they were well out of town. Even then he imagined seeing Conrad Burke on the road or riding up behind them or coming out of the bushes as the wagon bounced over the rutted road. Jack tried to keep up the conversation along the way, saying things like "There's a kangaroo!" or "I think I see the smoke from a paddle steamer through the trees," but Patrick couldn't think of anything to say back except "uh-huh."

"You sure you don't want us to drive you all the way to the

house?" asked Mr. Duggan when they arrived at the lane that turned off the main road.

"I'm sure." Patrick forced a smile. "Thanks for letting me ride along, Mr. Duggan. See you around, Jack."

He slipped off the wagon and tried not to limp until it was out of sight, then he stood still and listened. There was a crow, another bird he didn't recognize, and the nervous sound of a waiting horse.

Sounds close by, he thought as he limped down the quiet lane. When he reached Erin's Landing, he noticed the door to the cabin hung wide open.

"Ma?" he called. "Becky?"

Patrick heard a shuffling noise just inside the door, like an animal hiding.

"Becky?" he tried once more. "Ma? Are you in here?"

He took one step inside, and the door slammed shut without Patrick touching it.

"Bail up," commanded a man from somewhere behind him.

Patrick wasn't sure what "bail up" meant, but he understood the tone of the voice. He didn't move.

CHAPTER 9

UNWELCOME VISITORS

"Who's there?" squeaked Patrick.

"I said, bail up," barked the voice.

"It's all right, Patrick" came the comforting voice of his mother, only it sounded tight and worried in the shadows. All the curtains were drawn. "Just don't move, and do as the man says."

The man laughed as Patrick's eyes became used to the darkness. Someone was sitting on a box in the corner of the room, to the left of the front door. Almost without thinking, Patrick made sure his grandmother's ring was tucked safely under his shirt.

"That's right, boy," said the man, showing a yellow band of crooked teeth. "Bail up. Hold still. Just do as I say."

Patrick stared at the man's face—scarred and pockmarked, as far as he could tell, with dull brown eyes and a wild dark beard. The man hid under the brim of a crumpled brown hat and behind a serious-looking pistol that he kept pointed directly at Patrick.

"Where's your father, boy?"

"I already said, he's—" began Mrs. McWaid from the opposite side of the room.

"Quiet, woman!" roared the man. "I asked the boy."

Patrick finally glanced over at his mother to see her huddled next to Becky and Michael. They were standing by the bed, where another man was lying, deathly still. He looked hurt—bandaged around the shoulder with a ripped shirt, but still bleeding. His eyes were closed, and his head rested on the pillow. He looked younger than the bandit they faced, maybe only eighteen or nineteen years old.

"So, boy," the dark man with the gun cooed, "where did you say your father was? I just want to talk to him for a minute. That's all."

In the dim light from the window, Patrick looked again from the gun to the hurt man on the bed. "He's not here," he choked out at last. "We don't know where he is."

"You're lying, just like your mother." The man kicked at a wooden box on the floor and took a step toward him. "Don't try to tell me you're out here all alone. Your pa is outside hiding somewhere, isn't he?"

Patrick stared at the man. *He's closer to the truth than he knows.*

"Isn't he?" the gun came closer to Patrick's nose, and Mrs. McWaid stepped up.

"Leave the boy alone," she demanded. "We're telling you the truth."

"Why don't you believe us?" asked Michael, suddenly bold. "They put our pa in jail. He's not here."

Patrick froze while the man traced a line across his cheek with the end of the gun. Slowly a grin crept across the man's dirty face.

"In jail? Well, now, why didn't you say so?" He lowered the gun, as if a truce had been called.

"What do you want with us?" whispered Mrs. McWaid. The question made Patrick think that the two men must not have been there long before he stumbled in.

"What do I want with you?" echoed the man, turning to face Patrick's mother and sister. "I already told you, woman. Nothing, really. Just a safe place to rest and a little doctoring for my mate here. A traveler in need, and you're providing for him—a family of Good Samaritans."

Patrick shuffled to where his mother was standing, and the man twirled the gun on his finger.

"Ah, but I've neglected to introduce myself. Graham Simpson. Most people call me 'Hookey.'"

For the first time the man pulled his left hand out of his pocket and held it up for display. He touched the tips of his thumb and little finger together—there were no other fingers in between, only three little stumps. Becky gasped.

"Got into a disagreement with a fellow down on the river a few years back," explained the man. He made a chopping motion. "His knife was pretty sharp."

No one said anything, but the man on the bed groaned softly.

"Actually, I'm a businessman." Graham Simpson—Hookey—chuckled again, and it sent shivers up Patrick's spine. It wasn't the sort of laugh Mr. Duggan had. Not pleasant at all, but coarse and nervous. "You don't believe me, but I deal in gold, mostly. My partner here deals in lead. And you are?"

"You're not a businessman," piped up Michael, standing up straighter. "You're robbers."

"Robbers, eh?" Hookey pretended surprise, took a couple of steps, and bent down to look Michael in the eye. Then he hit himself on the side of the head as if suddenly remembering something. "Did you hear that, Wendell? The kid here thinks we're robbers."

The man didn't move, only groaned again.

Hookey nodded, then grinned. "Except in this country, little boy, we don't call them 'robbers.' We call them bushrangers. Sounds much more noble that way, don't you think? Haven't you learnt about the Hookey Simpson gang in your school?"

"We haven't started school here yet," replied Michael. Patrick jabbed his little brother with an elbow to keep him from talking.

Hookey nodded and held out his gun sideways as if he were a waiter presenting a dish of fine food. "Really? But you're a smart lad. You know what this is, then?"

This time Michael didn't answer, only looked away.

"And you know what it can do if it goes off—how it might hurt your mother or your sister? You wouldn't want that to happen, now, would you?"

Michael shook his head no while Patrick gritted his teeth. He could feel his ears heating up with rage.

"That's why you're going to do everything I tell you," continued Hookey slowly, "so your dear mother doesn't get hurt with a gun the way my partner did. Of course," he chuckled, "I expect your ma is a sight more clever than Wendell."

"What happened to him?" Mrs. McWaid looked down at the injured man. The only way Patrick could tell he was alive was by the way the man's chest rose up and down.

"Stepped in front of a trooper's bullet." Hookey shook his head and removed his hat in mock sorrow. "I should have left him behind, excepting that my sister's got herself married to him, and he's just a young kid, besides. Wouldn't be right, somehow, to leave your own brother-in-law behind."

"Why did he—" began Michael, before Patrick could jab him again.

"Because we were trying to do a little business with a Cobb and Company stagecoach," hissed Hookey. "And the trooper—excuse me, Her Majesty's law officer—riding on the top had the strange notion that we shouldn't have been doing that. Can't understand it, can you?"

Stagecoach robbers, thought Patrick, holding his breath. *Real stagecoach robbers. The ones Mr. Duggan told us about.*

"You're not right to involve innocent people in your crime," said their mother, but Hookey only smiled back at her.

"I'll make you a deal, ma'am." He pointed the gun straight at Becky. "Whatever your name is—and I don't really care what it is—you quit your preaching and doctor my mate, and we'll be off without any trouble to you. But if he dies . . ." Hookey pretended to pull the trigger and made a clicking sound with his tongue. "Doesn't it say somewhere, 'an eye for an eye,' something like that?"

Becky's lower lip trembled, but she remained still.

"I'm not a doctor," stammered Mrs. McWaid. "I can't—"

"Oh, but you can." His teeth clicked oddly when he spoke. "My dear old mother used to say that if you can't find a doctor, a woman is the next best thing. You don't blame me for taking her advice, now, do you?"

Patrick's mother reached down and felt the injured man's forehead, took a deep breath, and looked at her children with pain in her eyes. No one said anything for a moment.

"I'll do what I can," she finally whispered. "Becky, let's get his wound dressed properly. He's lost a lot of blood."

"Ah, I knew I'd come to the right place." Hookey grinned once more.

He looked around the inside of the little cabin, at the windows by the big ship's steering wheel, at the single door. Even though the pieces of the different ships had been nailed together in a crazy patchwork way, the house had only one floor. More important, there was no other way in or out than the single door.

"Strange place, this. Looks like some kind of riverboat. But last I knew, it was empty." He shrugged. "Ah well. Here we get a nurse in the bargain."

Patrick and Michael stood stiffly in the middle of the room while Becky and their mother tended to the man in the bed. Hookey paced nervously around the room.

"What are you good for, boy?" He poked at Michael with the end of his gun.

"I don't know what you mean," replied Michael. "I have to go feed my koala."

"Don't we all?" laughed the bushranger. "Yeh, and my kangaroos need a drink, too, while you're at it."

Michael looked to Mrs. McWaid for help. "I'm not kidding. I keep him in the box next to the house. He sleeps most of the time, but when he wakes up, he gets hungry."

"Tell you what, mate." Hookey crouched down and held the front of Michael's shirt in his free left hand. "You go get your koala and bring him back in here. That way, maybe we can all play with him."

When Hookey let go of Michael's shirt, Patrick's brother tripped over backward as he hurried toward the door.

"But you wouldn't run off, now, would you?"

"There's no need to be so rough, Mr. Simpson," objected Mrs. McWaid.

"Oh, so it's 'Mr.' Simpson now, is it?" The man repeated the words as if he had never heard anyone call him that before in his life.

Mrs. McWaid looked straight at the bushranger, her eyebrows set sharply. "As I was saying, Mr. Simpson, there's no need for bullying the boys about that way. I said I'd tend to your friend. You leave the children alone."

"Humph," said the man, but he turned away to check out the window.

"Is he going to die, Ma?" Patrick looked over his mother's shoulder at the wounded bushranger.

Mrs. McWaid could only shake her head. "I don't know, dear. Pray that he doesn't."

"That's right, boy," said the pacing Hookey Simpson. "Pray that he doesn't. My sister would never forgive me."

Patrick wondered at the man's words. "*You* have a family?"

"You think that's strange?" the man asked defiantly. "A sister and a mother and two little brothers. My old father even comes around once in a while when he's sober."

"Comes around where?" Patrick continued the questions. *If we can get him to talk about his family,* he thought, *maybe he won't be so mean to us.*

"Ballarat's where I grew up. Dad's a horse trader. Or was till he lost 'em all to thieves." Hookey got a far-off look in his eye, but he kept his pistol ready. "They sold the horses to the dirty government. Honest working man, my father was, till these good-for-nothing poms came and shoved us off our own land."

Patrick had heard English people called "poms" before, so he knew what the bushranger was talking about.

"Where's that little brother of yours?" asked Hookey, looking out the window once more. "He's not getting any silly ideas, is he?"

Becky shook her head. "He'll be right back."

Hookey frowned and continued with his story. "Yeh, well, as I was saying, dandies from London came and stole our land. I wasn't more than the kid's age at the time, otherwise I would've done something about it instead of waiting fifteen long years."

The man yanked open the door and shouted out. "Hey, kid, where are you?"

Michael didn't answer, and even Patrick began to wonder what was taking his little brother so long.

By that time the man's eyes were wild, racing about the room, and his voice got louder and louder. Patrick pulled back a step.

"I'll tell you this," continued the man, almost yelling back at them. "I've never taken a poor man's money, and that's the truth. Only fools who could afford it. You go to any town and ask about Hookey Simpson and his gang, and they'll tell you the same thing. We know everybody. People out here in the bush, they love us." Hookey waved his hands around the room, then watched for his audience's reaction.

"If people love you like you say," Patrick snapped back without thinking, "then how come the only way you can get them to help you is with a gun?"

Becky gasped at Patrick's question.

"Patrick!" his mother warned him. "Don't talk to the man anymore."

"Quite all right, ma'am," said Hookey, but his eyes narrowed with anger and his voice still held a hard edge. "The boy's entitled to his opinion. Now, what did you say, boy?"

He slid closer to where Patrick was standing, almost face-to-face, turned his head, and pointed to his right ear. "I don't hear so well out of the other ear no more. Gun went off next to my head once. So I'm missing three fingers *and* a little hearing, besides."

Patrick swallowed hard. He wasn't sure if the man was telling the truth, but he couldn't back down.

"Mr. Simpson . . ." Patrick's mother tried to referee, but he only waved her off with his gun, not taking his eyes off Patrick.

"I said . . ." Patrick gulped again. "How come you can only get help with a gun?"

The cabin was deathly quiet, then Hookey began to chuckle. The next moment he was laughing, then roaring, his head thrown back. "I like that, boy," he said, catching his breath. "You're not afraid of me, are you?"

If he only knew, thought Patrick, but he stuck his chin out. "I'm not afraid of you. You're not so tough."

Patrick shrugged his mother's hands from his shoulders and started to breathe harder.

"Oh, really?" Hookey didn't smell so good when he opened his mouth.

"Really. You think you're some kind of Robin Hood, but you're not. I'll bet you don't even know everyone around here the way you say you do."

The man arched his eyebrows, and his nose widened like a bull's.

Somehow Patrick kept pushing. Maybe he had a chance to learn something. "I'll bet you haven't even heard of John McWaid."

"McWaid." The man's eyes narrowed. "What do you know about McWaid?"

Patrick wasn't quite expecting that response, and he backed off. "Uh . . . you've heard of him, then?"

"There's a reward for his capture, boy. So if I knew where he was, I surely wouldn't tell you. Sit down."

"You know where he is?" asked Becky.

Hookey seemed to think for a long minute, then shrugged his shoulders. The fight with Patrick was over.

"Maybe I do," he said. "Maybe I don't. Now, what about my mate? Get on with the doctoring, would you?"

Becky and her mother returned to dressing the injured man's wound while Hookey resumed pacing. Patrick slumped down in his chair, wondering how he could have said what he said to Graham Simpson, the leader of the bushrangers. The man with his finger on the trigger of a gun.

I wonder if he really knows where Pa is, wondered Patrick.

"I see a paddle steamer coming!" announced Michael, running up to the front door with the baby koala on his shoulder. "They can see the house."

Patrick jumped out of his chair, glad for the distraction, but sat back down when Hookey glared at him.

"Hold it, kid," said Hookey, but Michael had already opened the door. "Did they see you?" he asked.

"I don't know." Michael held on to Christopher, who looked around the room with wide black eyes. The orphaned baby koala looked just like every drawing Patrick had ever seen of the Australian animals, with puffball ears, a thick coat, and a big black nose. He was cute enough to cuddle, but ever since someone had given him to Michael, the little animal would let only Michael pick him up.

"So go ahead and wave," ordered the man, fading back into the shadow where he couldn't be seen from outside the house or through the window. "Wave nice and friendly, like happy settlers, eh?"

The long, low steam whistle seemed to echo as it came closer.

"I'll bet it's the Old Man in the *Lady Elisabeth*," sang Michael. "Coming to check on us."

"Shh—" Patrick tried to quiet his brother, but it was too late.

"The Old Man?" Hookey perked up. "Who's that?"

Their mother looked up from bandaging the injured man with a touch of a frown, as if to say that they shouldn't have been talking about the paddle steamer or the Old Man. Outside, a boat went by on the river. Patrick knew it was too soon to have been the *Lady Elisabeth*, but . . .

Maybe this will help. Patrick had another idea.

"He's the fellow who owns this place." Patrick stepped over to the window and watched the smoke from the paddle steamer drift through the trees. It was not, of course, the *Lady E*. "He said he's going to be checking on us, come to see how we're doing."

"That so?" Hookey pulled the worn curtain out of the way to peek out the window, then paced around the room again before stopping by the bed. He never put down his gun, but he reached over to scratch Christopher's ears. "Cute little beast."

"The Old Man's a paddle-steamer captain," Michael put in, picking up on what Patrick was saying. He pulled away so Hookey couldn't touch his pet. "I heard someone in Echuca say he was an old codger."

Hookey missed the comment, frowned, and walked back over

to poke at the man in the bed. "Feeling well?"

"You know he's not," their mother answered for the injured man, who groaned as he tried to sit up straight. "You'll have to give him a chance to rest."

"I didn't ask you, woman," snarled Hookey. He poked at the man's bandages with the end of his gun. "I said, how are you doing, Wendell?"

"Never better," Wendell finally gasped, then gingerly took a sip of water from a glass Mrs. McWaid offered him. "Bullet just nicked me. But who are these . . ."

"Then get ready." Hookey's face was serious. "We're riding in a half hour."

The injured man coughed and sputtered while Hookey laughed. "Only joking, mate. I'll give you till morning to mend. This woman here volunteered to help. We'll leave after breakfast tomorrow."

"Oh, thanks so much." Wendell looked about weakly, obviously trying to figure out where he was, but Mrs. McWaid said nothing as she mopped his forehead with a damp towel. From outside they heard someone shouting.

"Is that your captain already?" Hookey demanded suddenly.

Patrick peeked out the corner of the window and groaned. "It's Jack," he reported. "He's coming back."

"What about Mr. Duggan?" asked their mother, rising up. Becky craned her neck to see out a window.

"Everybody down!" ordered Hookey, lowering his voice and swinging out his pistol once more.

Patrick crouched down next to Michael.

"Too many people around here," complained Hookey. "Too close to town."

He looked around the room quickly and pointed his gun at Patrick. "You, boy. Get rid of him."

"How do I do that?" Patrick asked.

"Just tell him to go home, that's all." The man opened the door slowly and started to push Patrick outside. "Just remember what happens to your ma and your sister if you say the wrong thing. No signals, no nothing. Just get rid of him."

"I'm going with him," said Michael, still holding on to Christopher.

"No, you're not." Hookey faded back into the corner where he had hidden before. "Just the older boy."

"I am, too," replied Michael, stubbornly pulling on his own shoes.

"Hallo, in there!" hollered Jack from out front. "Anybody home?"

"Go on, then." Hookey motioned with his gun, apparently too tired to argue with Michael any longer. "I'll be watching every move you make. Keep your friend out of here, whatever you do."

Patrick tripped out the door, not knowing what to say.

"Hey, there you are, Patrick, Michael." Jack held out a brown paper bundle and a small basket of brown eggs. "After we dropped you off, we got to thinking you should have this."

"Oh." Patrick heard a rustling behind him, and he looked back nervously at the door. Michael held on to his arm. "Thanks."

"Sugar too." Jack leaned closer and looked at the two brothers curiously. "Are you two all right? You look terrible."

"Thanks." Patrick took the gift and backed away. "I . . . ah, I have to go. Tell your parents thank you."

"Sure." Jack looked around the veranda as if someone might be hiding in the shadows, then stepped away with a puzzled look on his face. "I'll tell them."

Patrick took a deep breath, pulled his brother with him back into the cabin, and slammed the door. No one said a word until Jack had disappeared back down the lane.

"Ah, sugar." Hookey licked one of his hook fingers and poked it into the parcel. "Good job. Does your koala like sugar?"

Michael frowned. "Koalas only eat eucalyptus leaves. Everyone knows that."

"I'll cook something up for some early dinner," volunteered Becky, rescuing the sack. Minutes later a dozen eggs were popping on a skillet, and the smell seemed to revive even the injured man, who sat up in bed for the first time.

"You found your appetite so soon?" asked Hookey. "I thought you were dying a few hours ago."

Wendell grinned weakly. "Smells pretty good."

Patrick kept watch by the window as much as Hookey would let him as the others ate in shifts.

"Do you think the Old Man is coming back today?" asked Michael between mouthfuls of fried eggs.

"You better hope he doesn't." Hookey licked his lips. "Otherwise, he'll be like the constable in Swan Hill, who thought he was clever enough to get in the way of the Simpson Gang. Tell them what happened to that constable, Wendell."

"What?" Wendell had closed his eyes again, but he jerked awake when Hookey flicked a forkful of eggs in his face.

Hookey roared with laughter. "Wake up, Wendell," he teased his partner, who was hardly strong enough to wipe the eggs off his cheek.

"I can see your mother didn't teach you any—" began Mrs. McWaid.

"Ah-ah-ah, woman," interrupted Hookey. "Don't forget what I said. No sermons from you. And Wendell was just telling us about the constable at Swan Hill, weren't you, Wendell?"

"What about him?" Wendell's eyes were hardly open.

"You're not much of a storyteller, Wendell." Hookey leaned against the door, where he could see everyone at once.

"Obviously, he's not in any condition . . ." Mrs. McWaid's voice trailed off at Hookey's blistering stare. She turned to light a lamp instead.

"As I was saying, this wombat-headed constable tried to surprise us when we were in the town of Swan Hill, said he was going to lock us all up in his miserable little jailhouse." He laughed his coarse laugh again, and Patrick wished he could plug his ears.

"My children don't want to hear your stories, Mr. Simpson," protested their mother.

Hookey only rolled his eyes. "Well, and tell me, who do you think was sitting all alone in his own jailhouse?" He pointed at Becky. "Who do you think, young lady?"

Becky shook her head and looked at the floor. "I don't know."

"Oh, come on." He laughed once again. "What was even better was when Billy gets the idea to change clothes with the constable—Billy's my kid brother, see—and then he parades around the town streets like he was a visiting lawman."

He looked around the room and shook his head. "I can see you're not following the humor. Well, then Billy—his face isn't on posters everywhere, the way mine is, so people don't recognize him—Billy goes straight up to the front door of the constable's house and warns the fellow's wife to watch out for the Simpson Gang!"

"What did she say?" asked Patrick.

" 'Thank you.' That's what she said. Just 'thank you,' real proper. Didn't recognize the uniform or anything." Hookey erupted in laughter yet again, only stopping when he noticed that Wendell wasn't laughing with him.

"What's the matter with you, Wendell? You thought it was great fun, didn't you?"

Wendell didn't open his eyes. "Maybe it's the bullet that passed through my side, kind of changed my way of looking at things. After that last robbery failed . . ."

"Bah! I knew you were a fat-necked coward first time I laid eyes on you." Hookey took a bite of cold eggs and rolled them around in his mouth. "We're leaving in the morning, brother-in-law, whether you're ready or not."

"He's not strong enough for that," said Mrs. McWaid.

"Not my concern." Hookey set his jaw. "This place is busier than a Sydney train station. We're leaving before this Old Man shows up."

Mrs. McWaid just frowned while Hookey looked nervously around the cabin.

"I'll tell you what." He spied Mrs. McWaid's Bible on a shelf next to the bed and picked it up with a grin. "All you have to do is read a few words out of your book, and he'll be well, right?"

They all stared at him. Patrick didn't know what to expect next from the man.

"Here, you read it, sister." He threw the Bible at Becky. "Read me some magic."

"It's not a magic book," countered Becky, straightening a wrinkled page.

"Leave her alone, Hookey," whispered the man in the bed, but too softly for Hookey to hear.

"Read!" shouted Hookey. If Patrick hadn't realized it before, he knew then that the man was half crazy, or worse.

Becky looked rattled but glanced at her mother and then opened the book to the middle. She searched the page for only a second and took a breath.

"Psalm thirty-seven." Her voice was steady and strong, but Patrick noticed her hands trembled, and she kept her eyes glued to the page. " 'A little that a righteous man hath is better than the riches of many wicked. For the arms of the wicked shall be broken.' "

"I should have known," snapped Hookey, grabbing the Bible back from her. "A preacher, just like your mother. That's not what I asked you to read, girl."

With one hand he gripped the book, and with a grunt he tore it in half along the spine.

"There's what I think of your book, preacher girl." In the stunned silence he yanked open the door and pitched the two halves of the ruined Bible far into the bushes.

"You can't do that!" Michael was the first to react, and he launched himself against the bushranger with a howl. "That's our Bible!"

"Michael!" cried their mother, stepping up to rescue her son.

But Hookey only laughed as Michael tried to tackle his leg. He held the boy down while warning the others off with a shot through the ceiling.

The shot echoed through the cabin, locking even Michael into a statue pose. A puff of dust settled over their heads, and the sharp smell of gunpowder made Patrick blink. The koala hid under the bed.

"There, now, that's better." Hookey sneered at them and brushed Michael to the floor. Patrick helped his brother to his feet.

"You're a feisty crowd, aren't you? I think it's going to be bed-time early tonight."

Patrick put his arm around Michael as his little brother cried angry tears.

"We're going to escape," said Michael between his tears.

Hookey laughed. "I'll be sitting right here by the door waiting for you."

"Then I'll go out the window."

"I don't think so. You wouldn't want me to hurt the ones left behind."

"I'll just wait until you fall asleep."

"You try to escape, young man," threatened Hookey, "and you'll find out directly how awake I am. Now, quiet down and get to sleep."

CHAPTER 10

AFTER BECKY!

Patrick woke up to darkness. His mother, Becky, and Michael were in the hammocks above him, and Christopher was back outside in his box.

He wondered for a moment what had caused him to wake, and then he heard the faint whinny of a horse.

Who's coming? Patrick thought, getting silently to his feet on the cold wood floor. He looked at the bed where Wendell should have been sleeping, but the blanket was thrown to the side. He felt the mattress.

Still warm.

His mother stirred in her hammock, but no one else moved. He didn't hear a sound from Becky or Michael as he slowly turned the door handle and tried to keep the front door from squeaking on its hinges.

The dark shape of the bushranger was not at his station on the veranda.

Is he really gone? Patrick wondered. He shivered as he stepped into the dark, cool night air filled with the heady river aromas. He was about to turn back and wake his mother when he heard a horse again in the distance.

They weren't going to leave until daylight. Maybe they got impatient?

A sudden rustling in a tree above him made Patrick jump almost out of his shoes.

"Yow!" he cried softly, startled at the owl taking off a few feet above his head. He could almost feel the wings beating him in the face, and he wiped the cold sweat from his forehead with the sleeve of his shirt.

Another horse whinny told him that someone was probably untying Hookey's horses, so he quickened his step toward the grove of trees the noises came from. He heard soft voices and the sound of horses walking before everything became quiet.

Which way did that come from? Patrick thought he was going the right direction, but the horses must have been walking away from him, away from the river and the Old Man's cabin. He began to run.

Slow down! he almost whispered to the voices as he trotted through the brush. He wasn't sure why he was following them, and he wasn't sure he was heading in the right direction, either.

"Hold him up, would you?" Hookey's voice suddenly seemed as if it were right next to him, and Patrick stopped short. "He's flopping around like a rag doll."

"I'm doing the best I can," replied another voice.

Becky!

Patrick decided that he was almost alongside the horses, with the bushrangers just on the other side of a cluster of gum trees. In the dark, though, they could be almost anywhere.

"I'm fine, Hookey" came a third voice, softer even than Becky's. It had to be Wendell's. "Let's just keep going without the girl. I don't need her to hold me up. Fact, I don't know who's holding up who."

"I went to all that trouble to pull her out of the cabin without waking anyone up."

"All I'm saying—"

"You be quiet and keep riding," Hookey ordered. "A few hours ago you couldn't even sit up in bed, and now you're telling me you can ride?"

Patrick didn't hear Wendell answer.

"Besides, he's going to be hopping mad if we don't make it to Kangaroo Springs pretty soon. We're already way late as it is."

Patrick didn't know where Kangaroo Springs was, and he didn't know who would get mad if they didn't make it there soon. All he knew was that they were taking his sister, and he was not about to let them get away.

Determined, he padded along with the slowly moving horses, trying to hear more of what they were saying, trying not to break twigs as he walked, trying to ignore the pain in his tender ankle.

Been a few days since I fell on that ankle, Patrick told himself. *I thought it was better*.

The bushrangers kept going, picking their way through gum trees and overgrown brush for an hour or so, until the sky began to turn a soft pink. From somewhere in the branches above, a flock of cockatoos stirred up the crisp morning air. Any other time Patrick would have stared in wonder, but he hardly gave it a glance.

I should have gone back to get help as soon as I knew what was going on, Patrick scolded himself. *Ma is going to worry herself to death when she sees both Becky and me missing*.

The bushrangers stumbled through another shallow gully, then doubled back around a sand hill and took a new trail.

But if I did turn back, *I'm not sure I could find the trail again*.

By that time he saw the brown flash of a horse's tail through the brush. He froze. If he could see them, they might be able to see him, so he dropped back even farther. When he looked down to see if the horses left a trail, he couldn't see any hint in the soft carpet of eucalyptus leaves. Maybe it was a good thing that he hadn't wasted any time.

No, I can't take the chance of losing Becky, he decided at last. He looked around and realized that he was completely lost. The river was far behind them, the trees looked different—even the sun looked strange as it took its place and began to print long morning shadows on the forest floor. Trying to figure out which way to go, Patrick lost his footing and caught a root by his toe. A moment later he was flat on his face in the leaves.

"Hey, Wendell," asked Hookey, his voice echoing under a canopy of trees. "D'you hear that?"

Patrick lay still in the leaves, not daring even to flick off the ant that had found a way onto his nose.

"Just an animal," replied Wendell. Their horses had stopped, and one of them pawed at the ground.

"I don't think so," argued Hookey. "It was a crashing sound. Didn't you hear?"

"I didn't hear anything, Hookey." Wendell sounded tired, or maybe it was just because he was still weak and hurting from his wound.

Becky was silent.

"Hah!" shouted Hookey as a rock whistled over Patrick's head. "Get out of there!"

Another rock sailed past, then another. One nearly hit him in the side of the head, but he kept his nose buried.

Then he felt it—a fiery sting on his ankle, up his leg, two more on his stomach, and three on his face. Patrick screamed silently, forcing himself to keep his head still as an army of ants attacked.

Get off me!

He rolled slowly in the dirt, trying to snuff out the fire darts that now covered his stomach, but that only made the ants fiercer. Meanwhile, Hookey was whistling and whooping, not giving up his stone throwing.

"Hookey, I tell you, there's nothing there," groaned Wendell. "You're chasing ghosts. Or maybe kangaroos."

"Could we rest here?" Becky asked after a while. "I'm not sure how much longer I can keep holding up your friend."

Patrick tried to blow a flurry of ants off his cheek. He couldn't look up; Hookey and Wendell sounded as if they weren't more than a few yards away through the bushes.

Ow! Patrick bit his tongue, and his silent tears watered the dry leaves below his face.

"Hmm." Hookey sounded as if he was thinking it over. At least he wasn't throwing rocks into Patrick's hiding place anymore. "No, we keep going."

Patrick wasn't sure whether to feel relieved, but he knew he would have to get away from the anthill soon. After what seemed like an eternity, the two horses finally rambled away.

"Ohh," Patrick moaned and rolled to his side when he could no longer hear the horses. He looked up and, seeing no one, began madly swatting at his body.

"Ow, ow!" He swatted his belly and his back, his arms and his legs. He could still see the angry, swarming insects where he had been lying in the leaves. "Ow!"

But there's no time for this, he told himself, trying to sweep out the last of the ants from his hair. Everywhere, it seemed, his skin had been covered with the ants' fire and sting. He almost couldn't stand up straight from the pain.

In the distance, off to the right, he heard one of the bushranger's horses snort.

If I hurry, I can still catch up, he thought, pushing the pain aside and returning to the chase.

He followed the sound of the horses, at first crashing through the bush to catch up, then becoming quieter as he neared a smaller creek.

At least I can get a drink. At the bank of the creek, the water tasted cool and good and seemed to soothe his ant stings. He tried to drink extra to fill up his empty stomach. But since Becky and the bushrangers were still somewhere ahead of him, Patrick didn't dare stop long, taking only a moment more to splash water on his face.

Have to keep going.

For the first time since he fell, he looked down at himself and gasped. His pants were ripped through both knees, and his shirt had torn in several places. In between scratches, his arms were covered in red dots. He could only guess what his face looked like.

Can't stop now, he decided, running back up to the tiny trail the horses had made. He was getting to recognize it now. And now that the sun was rising, he was starting to regain his bearings.

He looked out over a more open prairie to his right, dotted with only an occasional lonely tree. To his left, the direction of the sunrise, the land began to rise. And straight ahead, the bushrangers seemed to be following the creek that ran like a snake through the thin barrier of forestland that lined it on either side.

Speaking of snakes—Patrick hastily checked the ground around him—*I'd better not run into any more*. He had completely forgotten about the possibility of stumbling on another snake since the one had caught on Becky's bootlaces the day they arrived at Erin's Landing. Trying not to think about it, Patrick simply followed the creek and listened for the horses that had to be just ahead.

"Hurry up, Wendell," complained Hookey. As he got closer, Patrick could again hear the bushranger's booming voice. "That's the third time we've had to stop since dawn, and we're riding slower than I can walk."

" . . . thirsty," mumbled the other man, and Patrick knew just what he was saying. By mid-morning, Patrick was ready for another break, too.

Breakfast sounds very good right about now. I wish I'd taken something to eat with me. His stomach began to protest even more loudly, and his feet seemed to be growing heavier and heavier.

Up ahead, the bushrangers had stopped to rest, and even from a distance Patrick could tell they were having something to eat. Patrick crept closer.

"Best bread I've tasted in a long while," grunted Wendell. He tore off a piece with his teeth.

"*Only* bread you've tasted in a long while," answered Hookey, chewing on his own piece. It had to be one of the stale loaves Mrs. McWaid had brought from town, about a week old and probably rock hard. Still, that sounded mighty good just about then. With a long knife, Hookey cut something off the side of a fist-sized ball and passed it around.

"Can't say we're not treating you proper," Hookey told Becky. "Cheese and bread . . ."

Patrick closed his eyes, hoping no one would hear his rumbling stomach. When he opened them, Hookey was adjusting his horse's bridle, and Becky was staring straight at Patrick.

She can't possibly see me, he thought, but he waved with a hand right in front of his face. Wendell wasn't paying attention.

"Mr. Simpson," asked Becky, "could I have some more?"

"Hungry, eh?" Hookey tossed the rest of a loaf of bread to her, and Patrick had to duck to keep from being seen. "Eat it while we ride. We've got a few more miles to go."

This time Patrick made sure he wasn't lying on an anthill while the bushrangers got back on their horses and continued down the trail. Patrick followed, almost stumbling over the gift Becky had set on a piece of bark behind a log.

"Breakfast!" whispered Patrick. Hungrily he picked up the food from his sister. He couldn't remember when a piece of stale bread and a slice of old cheese had tasted better, but he couldn't stop to enjoy it.

Thank you for the food, Father, he remembered to pray silently, and he trotted quietly down the path, following the two sets of hoofprints in the soft, dry earth. *And thanks, Becky*.

Around him the sun rose higher and started to bake the dry landscape with a bright yellow light. Only the winding creek to his left and the spindly trees that hugged the water offered relief. Like the bushrangers on their horses, Patrick kept to the shade and paused to drink when he was thirsty. Throughout the rest of the morning and into the afternoon, that became more and more frequent.

Difference now is that Becky knows I'm here. Patrick tried to encourage himself and to think of a plan. *But what am I going to do to free her?*

His mind went in circles, almost the same way he felt he was walking. He stopped for a moment in the shade, trying to keep at least one eye open to follow Hookey's and Wendell's horses. The next thing Patrick knew, he was jerking his head awake, and it was late afternoon.

What? I must have fallen asleep! Where are they?

He jumped up from his resting place in a grove of trees, looked around, and set off running.

This way! he told himself, following a couple of hoofprints in the dry, golden grass.

As far as he could tell from the sun, Patrick had been asleep for about three hours, maybe four. If he could have, he would have kicked himself for falling behind, for losing the trail. This time, though, he ran like a wild animal, flying through grassy fields and vaulting over tiny creeks that emptied into the winding stream on his left. Like a bloodhound on a trail, he tried to concentrate on the footprints, the broken branches, anything that would tell him where the bushrangers had taken Becky.

What did Hookey say the last time they stopped? Patrick tried to remember, but his mind wasn't cooperating. *Only a few miles left?*

He knew he couldn't keep running much longer. The nap had helped, but he wasn't sure when his body would collapse. Every breath hurt, and his legs felt as if he had strapped them to boat anchors. His ankle throbbed worse than ever. At last he slowed to a stagger and searched for the trail.

Where are their tracks? Patrick looked down at the dirt and panicked. The hoofprints were gone!

The trees were thicker now, and he could hear the sound of birds in the distance, behind a couple of sand hills guarded by a thick stand of trees.

Maybe I walked past their camp, he thought and turned to backtrack. A few hundred yards back he was standing by the hills. There in the damp earth he found what he was looking for.

Hoofprints! Patrick followed a fresh set of prints to the left, away from the stream, between two giant trees that seemed far too close together for a person to squeeze through, much less a horse. It was the perfect tunnel, shaded by trees in the front and covered over by trees above. When he had slipped through, he stopped for a moment to get his bearings.

This is it. Has to be. Kangaroo Springs.

Patrick looked around at the perfect hideaway. He couldn't even make out where he had come through the trees. A low, marshy gully ringed by trees opened in front of him, the ideal spot to hide a band of bushrangers. Little hills rose up on either side, boxing him in, and eucalyptus trees filled the gully with shadows.

But if this really is Kangaroo Springs, where are the bushrangers?

Patrick didn't have to wonder long. A whinny echoed off the walls of the canyon, and Patrick turned to see two horses tied to a tree by the hillside, contentedly munching grass.

It seemed every footstep would be heard, so he tiptoed toward the horses. Smoke hung heavy in the gully, and something smelled very good. Was it suppertime already? It was hard to believe he had been walking all morning and all afternoon, except for the time he had slept.

Suddenly the sound of laughing filled the gully, and Patrick jumped nearly out of his skin. It seemed to be coming from all around him, and he whirled around to place where the bushrangers were hiding.

That's Hookey, guessed Patrick, but he was confused. He couldn't follow his ears, and he couldn't follow his nose. So he just walked away from the horses, slowly making his way through the gully until he nearly fell into the camp.

"That's the funniest thing I've heard all day, Wendell," said Hookey. He was leaning over a fire pit, warming something in a cup. "You're not serious?"

On the other side of the fire, Wendell was propped against a saddle on the ground, and Becky was tied to a small tree at the edge of the clearing. Judging by the animal bones and rusty tools scattered around the clearing, this wasn't the first time the bushrangers had used the camp. Their black teakettle was bubbling furiously.

"Of course I'm serious," replied Wendell. "We don't have time to fool with her. Fact, I thought your Irish friend was going to be here waiting for us already." He sat up straight, and his voice seemed stronger than Patrick had heard before.

Hookey laughed again, and it echoed throughout the little hideaway. "Well, I did, too. He'll be here. And he's not going to be happy we haven't found his prisoner."

"Ahh." Wendell threw his piece of meat at the fire angrily. "It was all my fault."

"It was," agreed Hookey. "If it wasn't for you getting shot, we'd have a few hundred pounds of sterling jingling in our pockets from that stagecoach strongbox, and we'd probably still be on the trail of that escaped prisoner."

"But the girl . . ." Wendell pointed at Becky with his chin.

"Ah yeh, the girl," Hookey grew serious. "If we let her go, like you say, she'll lead the law back to our camp here before you have a chance to even stand up."

"Oh, come on, Hookey. We can't drag her around forever."

"Exactly. So do you want to get rid of her, or shall I?"

"I'll have no part in that. That's not what I came along for."

"Oh, so what exactly *did* you come along for?"

"You know perfectly well. First you told me we were going to make a bundle of reward money finding an escaped convict—"

"And we would have, if you hadn't gotten yourself hurt."

"Well, yeh, but that was the stagecoach robbery, which you didn't tell me about until it was too late, and which didn't work."

"Wasn't my fault you got yourself hurt."

"But I didn't say I'd go along with all that."

"Ah, but it's far too late for that, my brother-in-law. . . ."

As the men continued to argue, Patrick worked himself slowly around the edge of the camp to where Becky was sitting. He was covered by bushes for the most part, but not the last few feet. He would have to listen to them arguing until it got dark.

"Psst, Becky," he whispered.

At first his sister didn't move, but slowly she turned her head to look his direction. Even in the growing shadows he could tell her face was red and blotchy, streaked with tears. When she saw him, though, her eyes lit up.

"Patrick!" she whispered, glancing back at the two men. They were still arguing, and Hookey was getting louder as he paced in front of where Wendell sat.

Patrick didn't dare come any closer, and he put his finger to his lips. "Wait until it gets dark," he told her, ducking a little lower.

"Who made you royal governor?" Wendell shouted at Hookey. "If I want to go home, that's what I'm doing."

"I said no!" Hookey's voice was sharp.

Patrick backed away, deeper into the shadows.

At the campfire, Wendell reached out and kicked Hookey in the shin with his boot.

Hookey danced in pain for a moment, then came back at his injured brother-in-law. They rolled in the dirt, shouting and screaming at each other.

"Go ahead," said Wendell, lying on his back with his arms outstretched. "Take your best shot, *brother*. Hit me. Good thing I'm half dead, otherwise it might not be a fair fight."

"Bah." Hookey sat on top of the other man, gripping him by the neck. "I'm the one who saves your life, and you spit in my face. I should have left you to bleed. Why did I bother?"

Wendell didn't answer. He just lay in the dirt on his back while Hookey rose to his feet, dusted himself off, and turned back to the fire. It was getting darker, and soon Patrick would have his chance.

I just hope Hookey doesn't get his way soon, he thought, shuddering as he remembered the man's words about "getting rid" of Becky.

CHAPTER 11

PATRICK'S PLAN

"Not so close, Patrick," Becky whispered into the darkness without turning her head. "They'll see you."

"No, they won't," he whispered back. Patrick crouched just a few feet behind his sister, avoiding the flickering orange light of the campfire as it burned lower and lower. "They haven't seen me since I got here, and I'd say it's been three hours."

"Shh . . ." Becky glanced back nervously.

"All we have to do is wait until they're asleep, then I'll crawl up, untie you, and we're gone."

Suddenly Hookey's laugh rang out once again.

"You know, Wendell," shouted Hookey, drinking from his canteen. "You're going to make a great bushranger, as soon as you learn a few things from me."

Wendell only grunted and tried to brush the other man away. "What have I got to learn from you?"

"How to work the foreigners for a little more money, for one thing."

"Like your Irishman?"

"That's it." Hookey looked even more frightening in the firelight. "As soon as Conrad Burke gets here, I'll tell him you almost had his prisoner in your hands, but that we're going to need just a *bit* more cash to finish the job."

Conrad Burke!

"Did you hear what he's saying?" Patrick gasped to his sister.

Becky wiggled her wrists under the ropes. "I heard."

"It couldn't be."

"How many Conrad Burkes do you know?" asked Becky.

The answer was obvious. There was only one Conrad Burke. The same man who was after their father and who would stop at nothing to capture him. The man who had twisted the truth to make it look as if their father was the criminal, and that Burke was on the side of justice, when just the opposite was true.

"What I can't figure," said Wendell, "is where this Burke character is getting all the reward money. Why's he so concerned about capturing this poor fool of a convict?"

"You've got to learn not to ask those kinds of questions," said Hookey. "Just remember that Burke wants this fellow bad, and he'll pay plenty. We're the ones who are going to deliver the prize to our Irish friend."

Hookey grabbed an enormous knife and tripped over to where Becky was sitting, and Patrick held his breath, praying for a plan. Maybe he could jump out of the bushes and . . .

"Leave her alone, Hookey," Wendell said from his spot by the fire. "She's been through enough."

"My wrists are sore," Becky finally tried. "Can you untie them?"

"What did you say?" roared Hookey. "Speak up, girl!"

"I said, my wrists are getting sore. Can you untie them?"

Slowly Becky held out her hands. Patrick was afraid to look.

"Her wrists, Hookey," repeated Wendell.

Hookey jammed his knife into the side of a log and grinned. "What about her wrists? They're fine. I just thought she might like to come closer to the fire, away from the mosquitoes. Maybe recite some more of her Bible verses to us, huh?"

Hookey stepped over and gave Becky's rope a yank, and she cried out.

"Hookey, please . . ." Wendell had moved closer. He tried to undo the ropes around Becky's wrists.

"Leave her be!" roared Hookey, pulling out his knife again. "I want another sermon from the preacher girl. How about the one where I'm going to have my arms broken, eh?"

Hookey swung his knife in wide circles.

That's it, thought Patrick. *They're not going to hurt Becky any more.*

Without stopping to think what he would do if he hit him, Patrick picked up a rock nearly the size of his fist, aimed for Hookey, and let it fly. The rock sailed far over the man's head, though, and crashed in the distance.

Wendell froze. "What was that?"

"Burke?" called Hookey. He shifted the knife to his left hand, pulled the pistol out of his belt, and leaned out into the darkness. "Is that you, Burke?"

Patrick silently picked up another rock and heaved it as far as he could in the same direction.

You'd be in trouble if I were a better aim, he wanted to say, but he kept back in the shadows instead.

"We're over here, Burke!" Hookey pointed his gun into the darkness, and they listened. All Patrick could hear was his pumping heart, the whine of mosquitoes, and the crackling fire. Finally Wendell broke the silence.

"It's not Burke, Hookey," he said. "Just another animal."

Hookey wasn't giving up so easily. "Thought he'd be here by now."

"Maybe he gave up waiting and went out to look for us."

"If he did, that Irish city boy is going to get lost out there in the bush all alone."

Patrick crouched back down in the shadows. He tried to think of other ways he could rescue Becky; throwing rocks obviously wasn't going to be enough.

I could run through the camp screaming, he thought, swatting soundlessly at another mosquito. *Or maybe light a fire somewhere as a diversion.*

As he sat thinking, the bushes rustled behind him.

Patrick almost cried out, but he bit his tongue. He tried to see through the darkness around him, but he could make out only flickers of light from the campfire. He heard a snuffling sound somewhere at his feet and looked down to see the outline of a tiny creature.

The snuffling continued around him, then went toward the edge of the light. After a few seconds Patrick spotted an animal that looked like a hedgehog, odd and spiny, creeping in and out of the light, then stopping to eat something on the far edge of the clearing.

"There's that noise again," said Hookey, searching the shadows as he plunged his knife back into the log and picked up a canteen. "Did you hear that noise? It's the Irishman!"

"You're not talking sense anymore," replied Wendell. "And you're drinking all the water out of my canteen."

"Not your canteen," answered Hookey, holding the canteen behind his back with a smile. "Mine's empty."

"Get your own," roared Wendell. "Here I get myself shot for you, and still you steal my water."

He made a grab for his canteen, but Hookey ducked easily and tried to roll away.

"Come and get it." Hookey chuckled and rolled away from the other man, and they wrestled their way into the shadows.

There they go again, thought Patrick with a sigh, then he snapped to attention. Maybe this was the chance he had been waiting for.

"Give it, I say!"

The two men had disappeared into the bushes, and Patrick could hear Hookey chuckling. With not a second to lose, Patrick jumped to his feet and ran to the fire. He grabbed Hookey's knife out of the log and sliced the rope from Becky's wrists in one move. Neither said a word, but Patrick grabbed his sister's hand, and in a moment they had disappeared into the bush.

"This way!" he whispered, but in truth he wasn't sure which way to go. Any way that was away from Hookey and Wendell seemed fine. Becky didn't argue as they both sprinted through the darkness.

Faster! Patrick cried silently as they crashed through the bushes, stumbled, and fell. Becky helped him up.

Which way is the river? he wondered. They had missed the narrow entrance to the gully that led through the trees, so they just ran as fast as they could away from the light. From somewhere behind them, Patrick finally heard the roar he had been afraid of hearing, then gunshots.

"Keep running," Becky told him quietly. "I'm not going back there for anything."

Patrick nodded in the darkness. He would not, could not, let Becky down.

"You're not going to make it, girl!" Hookey roared in the distance, then another shot echoed all around them. For just a moment it sounded as if Hookey was in front of them, not behind. "We're going to hunt you down like an animal, and it's going to be worse than before."

"No, you're not," Patrick whispered back to the man, but he tried to save his breath for running. "I'm not going to let you."

Only trouble was, they were making too much noise crashing through the trees and bushes, probably leaving more of a trail than the horses had earlier that day.

"We should have jumped on their horses," panted Becky, but of course it was too late for that. Patrick wasn't even sure he would have been able to stay on one of the big animals, especially bareback. He kept running.

From somewhere behind them, Hookey kept up his yells. At times it seemed he was right behind them.

"Go ahead, then!" he finally hollered. "You'll never find your way home."

They kept crashing on, blindly at first, then with a better sense of direction.

"I think there's a little creek around here somewhere," panted Patrick. "If we can just find it, we'll know where we are."

Becky stopped to catch her breath. Somewhere behind them, though, Hookey followed.

"We have to keep going until we get far enough away, Becky."

"Uh-huh," she replied. "But which way?"

Patrick still couldn't find the creek. And he didn't want to say so to Becky, but he was completely turned around in the darkness. Maybe . . .

"Over this way," he said, trying to sound sure of himself. It was a different direction, he knew, but it had to take them to the water. The noise of Hookey following had faded behind them.

"Are you sure?" Becky sounded very small in the darkness, and Patrick wished he could see her face.

"I think so."

"Patrick . . ." She put her hand on his shoulder.

"We have to save our breath, Becky."

"I just wanted to say thank you."

"Plenty of time for that when we get back home."

"*When* we get back." Patrick said it again quietly to himself, to remind himself where they were going. *Home*, he reminded his legs as they jogged on. His mind wasn't thinking straight anymore, but they kept running, walking, running again. And still they didn't find the stream that would take them back in the direction they wanted to go.

"I don't understand it, Becky," Patrick mumbled at last. "I'm no good at directions. Seems like I'm always going in circles."

"What's that?" answered his sister. She had slowed to a walk again and was dragging her feet.

"I thought for sure we would find the stream by now."

"But we've been walking for an hour, haven't we? It's probably safe to stop for a rest."

Patrick took a deep breath. "Maybe we could stop. Then we could get going again in the morning."

He looked up ahead through the trees and noticed the faint flicker of a fire.

"Do you see that?" asked his sister. "Someone has a fire, up ahead."

"I see it!" Patrick straightened up. If they couldn't find the stream, they would find someone to help them find the way. Maybe someone with horses or a wagon. And something to eat and drink.

Patrick's mind swirled, and he almost couldn't stand as they stumbled toward the fire.

"Hello!" Patrick started to call out, but his voice didn't work. And then something registered an alarm in his mind, almost too late. Becky grabbed his arm from behind, and they fell to the ground at the edge of the camp.

"We're back where we started!" she hissed in his ear.

The horrible truth swept the cobwebs from his mind as Patrick looked around. His sister was right. Somehow they were back at Kangaroo Springs. It was hard to believe, and Patrick pinched himself to be sure, but there they were. The echoes proved it.

They could hear Wendell whimpering softly, then another voice—only this time it wasn't Hookey. They crawled up closer, and Patrick fought every instinct to run again. He wasn't sure if his legs would carry him. But that voice . . .

"It's Conrad Burke." Becky's whisper was flat, and Patrick knew she was right.

Burke. The man who was hunting their father, and now . . .

"This is a nightmare." Patrick shook his head and buried his face in his hands. "It has to be a nightmare. Nothing in real life could turn out this horribly."

In the light from the campfire, they could see Conrad Burke sitting on his horse and looking at Wendell with his dark-eyed vulture stare. He was still wearing his rounded bowler hat.

"What's wrong with you, man?" sniffed Burke. "I thought your brother told me in Echuca that you two were expert trackers, and that you knew where to find the Irishman."

"Well, sir, we ran into a bit of trouble on the way."

Burke looked down at Wendell sitting in the dirt by the fire and shifted in his saddle. He did not look comfortable on the horse.

"I can see that. So why weren't you here as we arranged?" asked Burke. "I swam my way out of a paddle steamer wreck just to meet you here the way we agreed, and you two *bushrangers* never bothered to show."

"Beggin' your pardon, sir, but as I said, we had a bit of an adventure ourselves."

"Hmm. You'll tell me about it, I'm sure. But what about the prisoner? Your brother promised you'd find him for me inside of two days."

"Brother-in-law," Wendell corrected him. "And we almost had him, but—"

"That's not good enough," Burke raised his unpleasant voice. "I hired you men to find a redheaded Irishman lost in the bush, and you can only tell me you almost had him? What's the matter with you?"

"It wasn't our fault," explained Wendell, shrinking back from the attack. "I don't know what happened to him. But he's not gone far. Don't worry."

Burke made no move to get down from his horse.

"What's so important about this fellow anyway?" Wendell threw another stick on the fire. "All this talk about a redheaded Irishman."

"Let's just say that my associate is very anxious for us to find this fellow. Some foolish guard let him escape before we could finish with him."

"Finish with him?"

"Never mind. You just worry about finding him. That's what I'm paying you for. My job is to make sure that McWaid never makes it back to prison to tell his stories. Understand?"

Wendell must have nodded, and Burke at last slid off his horse. He handed the reins to Wendell, who struggled to his feet.

"What happened to you?" asked Burke, noticing the bandages across the other man's chest.

"This?" Wendell stuttered for a moment. "Just a scratch. Caught a branch on the trail. I'm fine."

"Hmm. Well, then, where's your brother?"

"You mean my brother-in-law?" Wendell corrected him again.

"He's off in the bushes somewhere. Been chasing animal noises, thinking it was you."

A twig snapped behind Patrick and Becky, and Patrick smelled the overpowering bad breath of Hookey Simpson a split second before a strong hand clamped on his shoulder.

CHAPTER 12

DEN OF THIEVES

"Say, look what I've found here!" boomed Hookey.

Becky and Patrick both tried to squirm away, but Hookey's grip was incredibly strong. Becky cried out in pain as he locked his right arm around her neck.

"We started out with one." He twisted Patrick's arm savagely and dragged him toward the fire, and nothing they did slowed him down. "Now we have two."

Patrick tried to dig in his heels and turn around, but it was like trying to hold back a train. And even if he could somehow get free, he knew that Becky was still a hostage.

"Simpson," cried Mr. Burke, turning in surprise toward the scuffle. "What are you doing out there?"

"Just picking up a couple of apprentices for you, Mr. Burke." Hookey threw them both to the ground in front of the fire. "Looks like the boy followed us here from the cabin we stayed at last night. And they're Irish. Sound just like you."

Patrick looked up from the ground at Hookey, who grinned in triumph. He did his best not to look at Burke, but he already knew what the man would say.

"What an astonishing coincidence," said Burke. "Two of my favorite children in the world."

"You know them, Mr. Burke?" asked Wendell.

"Know them?" sputtered Burke. "Why, they're dear friends of the family. Their father, in fact, used to work for me as a reporter back in Ireland."

"Used to?" asked Wendell.

"Well, yes, until he began investigating several aspects of my business associate's personal life to a degree far beyond what was called for."

"What did he say?" asked Wendell, looking at his brother-in-law with a puzzled expression.

"The man stuck his nose into the wrong person's business," said Hookey, slapping his brother-in-law on the shoulder with the back of his hand.

"Ow!" yelped Wendell, gripping his wound. "That's where I was . . ."

Mr. Burke looked again more closely at the bandage.

"Uh, I mean, my scratch is still a bit sore." Wendell straightened up. "You know how scratches get."

"Certainly." Burke turned his attention back to Becky and Patrick. "Young Becky and Master Patrick." He shook his head and made a clucking sound with his tongue. "Regrettable that you seem to have involved yourself in this search for your father."

"You mean," sputtered Hookey, "this Irishman we're looking for is related? If I'd known that—"

"My father never did anything to you," Patrick blurted out, getting to his knees and looking up at Burke.

"Quite right," agreed Burke. He crossed his arms and took a step back. "He didn't. All he did was cause a great deal of trouble for the wrong man. And now look where that's brought us in this small world of ours."

"What are we going to do with them now?" asked Wendell.

Hookey laughed. "Wendell was thinking we could just let them go, Mr. Burke, after the girl almost got away, but I've been trying to tell him that won't work. Maybe you can talk some sense into him."

Burke chuckled. "He's quite right, my dear Wendell. It wouldn't do to have these poor children running loose in the bush. They might be harmed by wild animals. Why don't you secure them while we discuss the matter."

Wendell hesitated, and Hookey threw him a small coil of rope.

"He means tie them up," laughed Hookey, "until we decide how to get rid of them."

Burke put up his hand and took the rope himself. "Actually, I'd be quite pleased to do it myself. That way, I shall make sure these poor children are not harmed."

Patrick winced as the man tightened the rope viciously around his chest.

"Oh, I'm so sorry," said Burke. This time Burke's mask was off. Every time Patrick had seen him before—back in Ireland or on the trip to Echuca—the man had worn a thin mask of politeness. Now he tightened the rope with glee.

"In fact, I'm quite grateful to your father," Burke babbled on as if talking to old friends. "You don't understand, do you? If I'd stayed in Dublin, I would have lived and died there in that dreadful office. Now, coming here to find your father, I find I have new freedom."

"Some freedom," mumbled Patrick, squirming.

"Yes, imagine!" Burke breathed in deeply. "Here they'll believe I'm anything I say I am. Even a newspaper correspondent doing a story on the Australian colony."

Burke frowned at Becky and Patrick as he finished tying them up. "But then there's the continuing unfinished business with your father, I'm afraid."

"Why don't you just leave him alone?" asked Becky.

Burke shook his head. "Honor, my dear child. I was sent here for a purpose and paid a generous sum of money, by the way, to help preserve a friend's honor. Wouldn't you say that's a reasonable, respectable thing?"

Patrick and Becky didn't answer. Burke rubbed his hands together and studied his bushranger friends.

"Yes, honor!" he boomed as if delivering a speech. "The honor of a well-respected chief police inspector."

"Too bad he's a criminal." Patrick gritted his teeth.

"Let me tell you something, lad." Burke's deep-set vulture eyes flashed with fury, and he wagged a finger at Patrick's nose. "Your father is a meddlesome, misguided do-gooder who would have ruined a man's career. I did him a favor by arranging his transport here to Australia."

"Some favor," countered Patrick. "He was only after the truth. What did the inspector have to hide?"

"Bah! I'm debating a child." Burke pulled a handkerchief from his vest pocket, mopped his high forehead, and stepped back.

"Well, what *did* he have to hide, Mr. Burke?" asked Wendell.

Burke waved his hand as if to dodge the question. "You understand I'm not to blame for this situation. The problem arose when my friend found that merely sending McWaid away was no longer sufficient."

"Oh?" Hookey pulled at his beard, listening to the story.

"He grew concerned when someone else started asking questions. It then became my task to follow the prison ship and arrange for an accident to befall Mr. McWaid. Unfortunately, someone interfered—a guard, I think—and McWaid disappeared before I could locate him here. Quite unfortunate."

Burke picked up a smoldering stick by the fire and pointed it in the direction of the two bushrangers. "That's where you two fine gentlemen come in. Your job is to help me keep this obligation, and we'll share the rest of the money when McWaid is recaptured and—"

Patrick couldn't listen to any more. "You're horrible! You're even worse than they are!"

Burke only smiled as if he had been paid a compliment.

"You still haven't told us what we're going to do with *them*, Mr. Burke." Hookey waved toward Becky and Patrick.

Burke chuckled. "I haven't told you my grand idea, yet, have I? You two idiots can't seem to pull off a robbery on your own—"

"What are you talking about?" Hookey sprang to his feet. "We've—"

"Sit down, Graham," Burke interrupted him.

"People call me Hookey."

"As you like. But I know what the bandages are from. Just a tree limb, he says. I happen to know that Wendell was shot while you two were trying to rob the Cobb and Company stage recently."

"Well, what about it?" Hookey puffed out his chest.

"What about it?" Burke pulled out a pocket watch on a gold chain, checked the time by the light of the fire, and replaced it carefully in his vest pocket. "You fellows call yourselves the Simpson Gang, but you couldn't find a lost Irishman in the woods if he came up and asked you for directions. Now I have to come and personally supervise."

Wendell struggled to his feet, but Hookey held him back.

"If you weren't paying for this trip," Hookey hissed through clenched teeth, "I'd let my brother-in-law—"

"And what's more"—Burke looked the bushrangers straight in the eye as he interrupted—"you bumblers can't seem to rob a stagecoach, either."

Hookey and Wendell both glowered at the other man, but he only smiled. "Actually, you fellows are lucky I'm here to help you. And these two youngsters are going to add so much to the enjoyment."

CHAPTER 13

FINAL OFFER

"No matter what Burke says to us, don't answer," said Becky, turning her head to whisper into Patrick's ear. "The best thing we can do is stall until help comes."

"You really think help is coming?" Patrick whispered back. They were tied back to back only a few feet from the campfire, but the three men weren't paying attention to them.

"Of course it's coming," Becky whispered back. "You followed me, didn't you?"

"Just barely. I don't know if someone could find the trail if he didn't know what he was looking for."

"Hmm." Becky still sounded optimistic.

"What are they talking about over there?" asked Patrick.

Wendell looked their way, then turned back to the fire.

"For a while I thought Wendell was going to help us," whispered Becky, who was facing away from the fire but kept looking back over her shoulder to see what was happening.

"I thought so, too," agreed Patrick. "But now he's just going along with everything Hookey says, and Hookey is going along with everything Burke says."

"Did someone mention my name?" asked Burke, stepping over to where Becky and Patrick sat on the ground.

"Remember, don't say anything. . . ." whispered Becky.

"What was that, little lady?" asked Burke. "Speak up so we can all hear what you're saying."

Becky held her tongue.

"Oh, so that's it." Burke squatted down and gripped Becky's chin. "Strong and silent."

"Leave her alone!" Patrick cried as Becky jerked her face back.

Burke just laughed again. "I knew that would get a reaction from you, young man." He stood up and carefully dusted off his hands. Despite the horseback ride, his fine black pants still looked well pressed, and his matching bowler hat looked as if it belonged in a bank rather than somewhere out in the Australian bush.

"Maybe I'll just talk to you, lad, since it seems your sister is no longer on speaking terms with me." Burke circled around to Patrick's side, and though Patrick did his best not to look into the man's eyes, there was no avoiding him. Burke pressed his face closer.

"I don't have anything to say to you," Patrick blurted.

Becky nudged him in the back with her elbow, and Burke smiled. His teeth glimmered in the light of the campfire.

"Can't say that I blame you. But I have a deal for you. You understand deals, correct?"

"Not your kind of deals."

Hookey and Wendell guffawed, and Burke waved his hand for them to be quiet.

"All right, lad. You hate me. Frankly, I don't care much of that." *What does he mean?* Patrick wondered silently.

"Here's my proposition. You and your sister help us with a little business matter, and we'll let you see your father again. What do you say?"

"Don't listen to him, Patrick," said Becky. "He doesn't even know where Pa is."

Burke straightened up and looked around Patrick. "She speaks!"

"And she's right," added Patrick. "I'll bet you don't even know where my father is. Neither do those two."

"Those two?" Burke crossed his arms. "They need help, and

you're going to give it to them. But *of course* we know where your father is."

"If you knew," said Patrick, "why did you follow us to Echuca before, thinking we were going to take you to him?"

"And if you knew where he was," added Becky, "you wouldn't still be here."

Burke only laughed.

"You're not telling the truth," insisted Patrick. "You never did before. Why would we believe you now?"

"All I can give you is my word as an Irishman." Burke held up his right hand. "You help us, and I'll let you see your pa. That's my final offer."

Burke looked from Patrick to Becky. "But if you don't, I cannot guarantee what our two bushrangers would do, eh, boys?"

Hookey chuckled as he picked his teeth by the fire.

"What will it be?" asked Burke.

Becky set her jaw. "We're not going to help you with anything."

Burke looked straight at Patrick.

"You heard what she said," said Patrick, feeling braver.

Burke seemed untroubled by their answer. "You'll change your mind when you get a little more hungry," he said, turning back to the others. "I brought you something, boys. Take a look at the beef in my saddlebag."

Before long, the campsite was filled with the smell of fresh meat roasting over the fire, a terrible, wonderful smell. Patrick closed his eyes from seeing, but he couldn't close his nose from smelling. He knew that he couldn't keep going without food, and Becky had to be starving, too.

"You must be hungry, boy." Hookey held up his plate and chewed his food noisily. "Why don't you come over and join us?"

Patrick shook his head, but just then his stomach let out a rumble that could be heard all over the camp. The men laughed.

"He says he's not hungry," teased Burke. He walked over to Becky, waving his full plate of beef in front of her face. She closed her eyes and tried to ignore him. "And neither is she."

A crashing sound in the bushes interrupted them. Patrick knew right away it wasn't an animal, and Hookey pulled out his gun.

"Coo-ee!" whooped someone from the darkness. Hookey smiled and put down his gun.

"It's Billy and the others," he told them, then he cupped his hands around his mouth. "Billy! Over here!"

A minute later the camp was filled with loud men: a tall, awkward-looking boy in his teens; a scar-faced fellow called Jim; and a third man who almost disappeared into his hat. All three members of the Simpson Gang wore blue wool shirts, heavy cotton trousers, and crudely sewn knee boots. Ponchos strapped on in front as knapsacks, and crumpled brown felt hats completed the "uniforms." They all filed past Patrick and Becky as if the McWaids were a new zoo exhibit.

"What have you got here, Hookey?" asked the skinny one with the big hat. "Couple of new gang members?"

"Yeh, these are the kids who are going to help us tomorrow," boasted Hookey after he had slapped all his friends on the backs in greeting. "It was Mr. Burke's idea."

"Conrad Burke." The Irishman shook the hands of all three newcomers. "I'm the one who's paying you the bonus to find that escaped prisoner, remember?"

"Ah yeh," said the youngest one. "Hookey's told us about you." Hookey introduced the others.

"This is my younger brother, Billy." He waved at the boy, who fell over backward when he tried to sit down. "He's a little awkward, but at least he's not got himself shot yet. Fella with the scar on his nose is Jim, who's just gotten out of the Wagga Wagga jail. And the skinny one is Charlie Johnston. If he turns sideways, you can't see him."

Charlie Johnston obliged by turning sideways and holding his arms in the air. Sure enough, he was probably the skinniest man Patrick had ever seen.

"But really, Hookey," asked Billy. "Tell us about these kids."

"A long story, mate." Burke put his arm around Billy and led him to the fire. The others huddled around and helped themselves to the meat. Patrick couldn't make out what they were saying, but in a moment they were all laughing together. Charlie Johnston, the skinny one, looked over his shoulder at Becky and Patrick with a nervous grin on his face. It seemed to Patrick he had seen that kind of grin before; it reminded him of the look on a bully's face as he was tying a can to a cat's tail.

"I like it," said Charlie, and the others laughed again. "Good plan, Mr. Burke."

CHAPTER 14

SECRET MEAL

Patrick was sure he heard horses in the night, but when he woke up, all he could hear was his sister's regular breathing. He tried to get comfortable one more time.

"I can't sleep sitting up like this," he whispered to no one in particular. The campfire was only a dim orange glow, and Patrick shivered in the cool of the evening. He counted five shapes sleeping around the fire: Wendell and Hookey and the three other members of the bushranger gang, Billy, Jim, and Charlie. Burke was off by himself, closer to the horses, wrapped in a pile of blankets.

"I can't sleep, either," sighed Becky. "I've been counting the stars for the past hour."

"Praying?"

"Yes," replied his sister. "I'm scared, too. Ma is probably worried sick."

"I wish someone would find us."

"I still think someone will."

"You're optimistic. And my stomach hurts, it's so empty."

Patrick knew that if he started talking about his stomach or about food, he could describe it in detail. He had never imagined being so hungry. His mind wandered, and he thought about the Old Man and the *Lady Elisabeth*, about Jack and their time at the Echuca wharf. . . .

"I have an idea how to get some food," he finally whispered.

"I'm listening."

"All we have to do is scoot closer to where they're all sleeping and get the rest of the food in Burke's bag. I saw him put something in there. We can stand up, kind of like the stick game the boys were playing on the wharf back in Echuca, only backward."

Becky didn't say anything for a minute, as if she were considering the plan.

"I remember," she said at last. "Stick. Ready?"

"Ready."

"Okay, plant your feet in front of you, then push up and back. One, two . . ."

Patrick planted his feet as his sister had told him, and they rose slowly at first until Patrick's sore right foot slipped and they tumbled.

"Ow!" whispered Becky. They lay still in the darkness, not daring to move a muscle. Someone snorted over by the campfire.

"I don't think they heard us," Patrick whispered back after a while.

"Okay, then." Becky rolled back upright, carrying Patrick with her. "Let's try again. Slowly."

This time Patrick was facing the sleeping bushrangers, and he did his best to push up without making a noise. A moment later they were standing up.

"Good." Becky checked over her shoulder to make sure Patrick was all right. "You with me?"

"Right behind you."

"Let's turn sideways and walk like crabs."

They did, inching their way closer to the snoring men around the campfire. Hookey snorted again, and they stopped short. He was holding his gun loosely in his lap.

"Don't move," ordered Becky, but no one seemed to notice them.

"I'm going to take Hookey's gun," Patrick decided, bending down to see how close he could get to the bushranger. "Throw it into the bushes. Then we can run."

Becky pulled back. "No, you're not!" she hissed. "Too danger-ous."

Hookey shifted and gripped his pistol in his hook hand, holding it closer and smacking his lips.

"Hold it," mumbled the man.

Patrick froze, but Hookey didn't open his eyes.

"He's talking in his sleep," whispered Becky. "Come on."

They crab-shuffled to where Burke was sleeping. His open knap-sack was at his feet, half filled with strips of leftover dried-up beef, partly wrapped in several white handkerchiefs. Patrick knew what it was just by the smell.

"All right," Becky whispered instructions again. "We lower our-selves down again, and then we can reach the beef."

Patrick nodded, and they fell to the ground while Burke snored contentedly a few inches away.

"What if he wakes up?" Patrick wondered, but Becky had no answer. They leaned closer to the pack, and Patrick reached out as far as he could with his left hand.

"Got it," he whispered, and they dragged their dinner back to a safer distance, a couple of feet away.

"Can you reach anything?" asked Becky.

Patrick unwrapped the cloth. "Wait a minute."

"Shh," Becky warned him.

Patrick tried to reach down but could only groan.

"What's wrong?" asked his sister.

"I can't get my mouth down to my hand. See if you can."

Becky did the same thing, but they only ended up in a heap on the ground.

"Look," Patrick finally said, "the only thing that's going to work is for us to eat like . . ."

They both crawled up to the knapsack face-first, and Patrick grabbed the opening in his teeth.

"Like dogs," his sister finished the sentence.

Well, I'm hungry enough, he told himself, biting off a mouthful. They used the sack as a sort of table.

He and Becky ate quietly until they had finished most of the meat. Becky even found a small canteen, so Patrick nibbled off the cork and they took turns lapping up as much water as they could before it all disappeared into the dust. With the edge of his hunger pain gone, Patrick's mind cleared a bit.

"Think we can make it out of here before someone wakes up?" he whispered, trying to swallow a mouthful caught in his throat.

"As long as we don't get lost again," answered Becky.

Patrick tried to straighten out, again sitting up with Becky. For the first time in what seemed like days, the pain in his stomach was gone, but something sharp and hard poked him in the shoulder.

"Had enough?" asked a quiet voice.

Patrick looked behind them to see Wendell's dark figure towering over them, the long barrel of the man's gun planted squarely between Patrick's eyes.

CHAPTER 15

BURKE'S SURPRISE

"Please," whispered Patrick. "We were hungry."

"So I gathered," whispered the man. "I've been watching you down that food for the past ten minutes."

"We weren't trying to cause any trouble," added Becky.

Without another word Wendell reached down with his left hand and pulled them to their feet, then dragged them back to their spot away from the fire. When his face was closer, Patrick thought he saw the man grimace in pain.

"Are you all right?" asked Becky.

"What's going on, Wendell?" asked one of the others.

"Just a couple of animals trying to get into our food," replied Wendell. He picked up Burke's half-empty knapsack and tossed it onto the older man's feet.

"Huh?" Burke snorted and jerked but didn't completely wake up.

"Go back to sleep," Wendell told them as he settled back to his own place. "Big day tomorrow. And don't get any more ideas. We're even now."

Patrick noticed that Wendell didn't lower his gun; it was cradled between his two boots, sticking out between the folds of his thin blanket.

"We should have run first, then tried to eat," Patrick whispered to his sister. He felt her shake her head.

"No. He was watching us the whole time."

Patrick sighed, and he knew his sister was probably right. And now, with Wendell's gun pointed straight at them, he could hardly close his eyes, much less fall asleep.

Big day tomorrow. The man's words echoed in Patrick's mind. What did Burke and the bushrangers have in mind?

When the sky began to lighten hours later, the gun hadn't changed position, only bobbed in time to Wendell's steady breathing. And Wendell still stared at them with large, unblinking eyes.

Ha-ha-ha! came a screeching sound that split the morning stillness. Patrick would have jumped out of his socks if he and Becky weren't still bound together.

"What was that?" cried Burke, throwing his blankets up in panic and scrambling to his feet. The other four men hardly rolled over.

Ha-ha-ha! came the sound again, from high overhead in the crown of one of the taller trees nearby.

Burke spun in panic, grabbed his pistol, and fired into the trees. Wendell and the other men only laughed.

"How long have you been here, Irishman?" asked Hookey from his bed. "Haven't you heard a kookaburra in the morning?"

Burke snorted and replaced his gun in a small holster on his side. "Of course I've heard a kooka . . . er, kooka-burro."

"Kookaburr-*ah*," Hookey corrected him.

"You call it whatever you like." Burke cleared his throat and pulled out his pocket watch. "In the meantime, it's six o'clock. Don't forget, our appointment is at nine, gentlemen."

The others groaned when Hookey kicked at them on the ground. Billy even reached out and grabbed his older brother's feet, and they wrestled for a few minutes before Burke stepped in.

"Enough of that, now, boys. We have work to do, and the sooner we get it over with, the sooner we can get to the real business at hand."

Billy stared up from the ground. "Which is?"

Hookey hit his brother on the side of the head, and Billy howled in pain. "Come on, Billy. He's talking about finding his prisoner."

"Boys, boys," said Burke. "I didn't hire you to beat each other up. Just to find the Irishman. Our job here this morning is only a bonus so we can get a bit of extra spending money. Understand?"

The others nodded, and Burke turned to Patrick and Becky. "What do you say we untie these two so they can earn their keep?"

"I need my horse saddled," offered Wendell, chewing on a stale piece of bread.

After Charlie untied them, Patrick rubbed his wrists for a moment before he got to work saddling horses. He noticed that Wendell never took his eyes off them, and he never lowered his rifle, either.

"Hold it steady, man!" Burke was carefully shaving over a bucket of water by the fire, his chin and cheeks covered in white shaving lather. He had recruited Charlie Johnston to hold his mirror, and the young man stood looking into the air as Burke scraped his cheeks with a razor.

"Come on, come on." Hookey slapped Patrick on the back. "We've got to ride in a few minutes."

"Where are we riding?" asked Patrick.

"When are you going to let us go?" asked Becky.

"Questions, questions. Hey, Burke, why don't you tell your friends what they're going to be doing today?"

Burke dabbed his face delicately with a small linen towel from his knapsack and turned to the bushrangers. "Not until it's time, boys. But come here, and I'll tell *you* something."

The others gathered around.

"We're meeting someone at nine this morning," explained Burke, "and since they're not expecting us, I want you to look your best." He frowned at Charlie. "Tuck in your shirt, son. You don't want anyone to think we're a dirty bunch of bushrangers. People would get a poor first impression."

The others laughed while Patrick and Becky held the horses, but Charlie even slicked back his hair, too.

"Those two need something to eat," Wendell finally said, picking up another piece of bread.

Burke waved at the bubbling black teapot on the fire. "Certainly, go ahead, children. We're not such a hard bunch."

It had been only a few hours since they had eaten their fill from Burke's backpack, but Patrick and Becky wasted no time helping themselves to dried toast and hot, smoky tea from the black pot. Patrick smiled as the tea warmed him up inside.

"So here's what we do. . . ." Burke again lowered his voice, the way he had the night before at the campfire. He took a few steps back and gathered the others around him, then acted out something with his hands. He drew pictures in the dust with a long stick, pointing out each of the bushrangers in turn, even Becky and Patrick. Finally, he dismissed them with a clap of his hands.

"Are you sure you can make it, Wendell?" Hookey turned to his brother-in-law as the others mounted their horses.

Wendell frowned and grabbed the reins of his horse. "I don't need any girl to hold me up, if that's what you mean." With a grunt he slid up on his saddle.

"We're not going, whatever it is you're doing." Patrick thought he would try again to defy the bushrangers. "And you can't make us."

Burke only laughed, as if Patrick had just told a joke. Becky was forced to ride behind Billy Simpson on his black horse, and Patrick was pulled up by one arm behind the surprisingly strong and wiry Charlie. Burke and Hookey led the way out of the gully, back through the narrow opening between the trees. Charlie and Billy guided their horses through the opening behind the leaders, followed by Wendell and the scar-faced Jim in the rear.

"Don't worry about a thing, kid," Charlie called over his shoulder at Patrick in a loud voice. He sounded friendly for the first time since he had arrived at the camp. "We'll be back here in just a few hours."

"Charlie!" Hookey warned the other bushranger sharply. "Keep your mouth shut. You want to announce it to the whole world?"

"Aw, come on, Hookey," replied Charlie. "You act as if the bushes could hear us."

Hookey only grunted in reply.

"Can't you tell us what this is all about?" Becky asked.

Billy didn't answer, but Patrick looked over and thought he saw him grinning.

Why such a secret? Patrick wondered, along with a hundred other questions. Where were they going? Why were they being dragged along with these men? What good could they possibly do now?

"Low bridge," said Charlie as a branch caught Patrick in the forehead before he could duck.

"Ow!" Patrick rubbed his head. From then on he paid more attention to the low-hanging trees that caused them to duck every few miles. But if Burke had been right that morning about meeting someone at nine, they wouldn't have far to go. Just then the overcast sky opened up and began to let loose a steady drizzle.

"Are you going to tell us where we're going yet?" Patrick asked an hour later. He was completely soaked.

Charlie shook his head. "Can't tell you anything until the boss does."

Patrick sighed and looked over at Becky, who gave him the same wet shrug. Her blue dress looked heavy with water. Up ahead, Patrick thought he saw a slight clearing in the trees, then a set of muddy wagon tracks. They hadn't seen another human all morning, not even a cabin.

"This is it," announced Hookey, pulling back the reins and sidestepping his horse so the others could pass. He pulled out his pocket watch and looked at Burke. "Right on time, Mr. Burke."

Burke mopped his wet forehead with his handkerchief, nodded, and looked around. "It's just as you described it, Mr. Simpson—er,

Hookey. Lots of rocks and hiding places. Narrow road. Yes, this will do quite nicely."

"And nobody around for miles," added Hookey, waving his hand around.

"Fine," agreed Burke, "but right now we'd better get into position before our guests arrive."

Billy, Jim, and Charlie looked to Hookey for direction, but he just nodded. "It's all right, boys. You do what Mr. Burke says. Remember who's paying the bills this trip."

Burke beamed and slipped off his horse, then tied it to a tree with the rest of them. "This is marvelous," he bubbled, but no one listened. "What a story this would make!"

Hookey turned to the others and checked his rifle. "Out of sight, boys, and remember to shoot over their heads first."

Shoot over their heads! Patrick looked at his sister, and he hoped he didn't look as scared as she did. He had a pretty good idea what was going on by then. The wagon tracks belonged to the regular Cobb & Company stagecoach that had to be coming their way.

"Why don't you let us get out of here?" asked Patrick. "We're not going to help you rob the stagecoach."

Hookey and Burke dragged them to the middle of the wagon road, let them go, and stepped back.

"Ah, but that's where you're wrong, my dear boy." Burke chuckled. "You and your sister *are* going to help us, and now I'll tell you exactly how."

"Why don't you just leave us alone!" cried Becky.

Burke shrugged defensively. "Exactly what I propose to do. We leave you here, and when the stage comes, you just wave all you want. Get it to stop for us. Have a nice chat with the people on board if you like."

"What if we don't?" asked Patrick.

"I've asked our friends to keep you in view." This time Burke didn't sound friendly anymore. "And they're very good shots. I suggest you don't move from your spot here in the middle of the road. We want to avoid any unfortunate consequences. Is that clear?"

Patrick knew what he meant. It was the same as if they were

tied up with ropes back at the campsite.

"And quit crying, girl." Burke sounded irritated. "Did you hear what I said?"

Becky nodded.

"Mr. Burke," Billy called from his hiding place behind a tree. "The stage is coming this way!"

"Perfect." Burke backed away from where Becky and Patrick still kneeled in the mud. "Just keep your wits about you, and no one will get hurt. I wouldn't want your mother to worry."

What is Burke saying? Patrick wasn't sure whether to laugh or to cry, so he helped Becky to her feet.

Hookey grabbed the other man's arm. "Come on, Burke, leave it now. We have to—"

"Yes, yes." Burke acted as if they had plenty of time. "Now, children, don't forget I'm a man of my word. And I promised to let you see your father in exchange for your help."

"'Course," added Hookey, "you didn't say whether that would be alive, or otherwise." He launched into a gale of laughter, and Burke pretended to be annoyed.

"Quiet now," Burke scolded the other man. "You're ruining the surprise."

Burke and Hookey disappeared into the bush without another word, and Patrick looked around them in the drizzle. There was no way out, no way to escape the men. He could only hear their low voices as Hookey checked to make sure they were all in their positions.

"You ready, Billy?" called Hookey.

"Ready" came Billy's voice from somewhere in the trees.

"Jim?"

"Here."

"Wendell?"

"Yeh."

"How about you, Charlie?"

"All set, boss."

Lord, Patrick prayed, his head down, *how did we get into this horrible mess?*

CHAPTER 16

THE HOLDUP

Patrick couldn't make his brain think fast enough. Run and hide before the coach came? He remembered Burke's threats, and he knew the man was serious. Run and stop the stage before it got this far? They were running out of time.

"It's too late, Patrick," said Becky.

As they stood in the middle of the road, rain dripping off their faces, Patrick knew she was right. Too late. They waited as the cheery red stagecoach pulled by six speckled gray horses raced around a bend in the road. Mud spun from the wheels and flew up from the horses' hooves, covering the coach and the two men sitting up front. By that time Patrick knew the driver had already seen them.

"Hold it, whoa!" cried the driver, pulling back hard on the reins. Like the man sitting next to him in the front bench seat, he was wearing a full black all-weather coat and a wide-brim hat. They looked down, concern and mud specks all over their faces.

"What in the world are you two kids doing out here?" asked the driver, a young man with a very American accent. "You look like a couple of abandoned kittens."

"I'm sorry," began Becky.

"Go back," croaked Patrick, springing to life. "Turn around!"

But he knew there was no way the stagecoach could turn

around, not in this narrow roadway. That was, after all, why Burke and the bushrangers had chosen this spot. And they were hiding only a few feet away, with their guns pointed straight at them.

"Say," called one of the passengers, pulling back a canvas window flap, "what's the delay, driver?"

"Seems we've got a couple of lost urchins out here," replied the bearded driver in a kindly tone. The horses gave their reins a shake as he climbed down out of his seat. "That's okay, Gray." He soothed one of his horses with a pat on the back.

"Don't—" Patrick began, but he didn't know what to say. *Don't, or do?* He held out his hands.

"What?" The man looked at them sideways, the way a dog does at a strange sound, and Patrick could tell the man suddenly sensed trouble.

"They made us do it," said Becky, stepping in between the horses and the stage. By that time a couple of the passengers were hanging out the windows, braving the rain.

"Are they hurt?" asked a woman. "Do they need a doctor?"

"Who made you do what?" asked the driver. He took off his coat and placed it around Becky's shivering shoulders, but her dress hung like a wet rag on her. "Here, why don't you get out of the rain?"

"No need for that," said Hookey, stepping quickly out from behind the stage. He pointed his revolver squarely at the driver's chest. "She's just fine."

The driver's jaw dropped, and he looked back quickly at his partner, still up in the driver's seat.

"Don't fight us," Hookey warned him. "My men are all around you. Just do as we say, and you'll live to see tomorrow."

"I'm sorry," repeated Becky, covering her face. "We're not part of them."

The driver looked from Becky and Patrick, then over to Billy and Jim, who had taken positions around the stagecoach and in front of the horses.

"No," he said, holding his shaking hands in the air, "I can see you aren't."

"Quiet, please!" yelled Hookey. "I'll be the one to conduct this transaction. Now, everyone kindly step out of the coach, if you would, please."

Slowly the door swung open, and a sad parade of six well-dressed men and three women stepped cautiously out into the rain and mud.

"See here," protested the first man out, the older man who had been complaining about the stop.

"Get out of there!" yelled Billy, waving his pistol dangerously close to the man's head. "You heard what the man said."

"Now, now, Billy." When Hookey scolded his younger brother, he sounded almost like Conrad Burke. "No need to be rude. Watch your step there, ma'am." He put out a hand, which an older woman in a frilly yellow skirt and lacy blouse refused.

"It's all right, Mrs. Weaver," said the driver. "We have to do as he says."

"Very good, sir." Hookey beamed. "No heroes, no one hurt."

No one said anything, just stood stiffly in the rain, and Hookey strutted up to the passengers.

"Well, then, you may all be wondering why we're all standing out in the rain gettin' wet like this. Unfortunately, I have to trouble you for all your cash, please, as well as your watches, rings, and purses. My friends are going to come around with a leather pouch for your things, so you just hold still for a few minutes."

Burke appeared from around the other side of the coach and tossed a sack at Patrick. He had strapped a neckerchief around his face as a sort of mask. Patrick looked at the empty leather pouch and shook his head.

"You collect your own," said Patrick, dropping the sack in the mud.

"I see you still don't understand, kid." Hookey's voice grew as cold and hard as the polished gray metal of his revolver. "So let me put it this way. Now that you've done your work, you and your sister aren't so useful to us anymore. And you know I'm not afraid to use this gun. But I won't harm *you* first. I'll start with your sister here."

Becky backed up against one of the horses, but there was no

escaping the bushranger's threats.

"Now, pick up the sack and get to work, or do I have to show you what I mean?"

"You can't help it, boy," said a man, the first in line. He slipped a wedding band off his finger and held it out. "Here, take it."

"Smart fellow." Hookey smiled. "'Course, it just hurts me to see the trouble I'm causing you."

Patrick sighed, looked over at Becky, and picked up the sack. He couldn't bring himself to look in anyone's eyes, though, as he shuffled past the lineup of passengers. All he saw were the people's hands as they emptied their pockets of gold coins, watches, diamond rings, and bundles of money. Shaking hands, mostly. Trembling hands, like his own. At least the rain was letting up.

"You, there!" Hookey pointed his gun up at the second driver, who hadn't yet climbed down from the driver's seat. "I'll need you to bring down the mail sacks, nice and easy. We'll do our best not to disturb them more than necessary."

The man nodded nervously and came down with three bulging canvas sacks, which Billy took from his hands when the man took up his place in line with the other passengers.

"Don't you have anything else?" Hookey leaned over to search the vest pocket of an older man, who had just dropped a small handful of sovereigns, or gold coins, into the leather loot sack.

"That was given me by my father. . . ." The old man's voice shook as Hookey pulled out a small gold watch on a chain.

Hookey bowed and snapped the chain off at the end with a jerk. "And we'll be so careful to take good care of it, mister."

Next was an old woman who had been crying in fright the entire time of the holdup.

"Now, now, dear woman," crowed Hookey, patting her on the back. "Don't fret yourself so. We'll be long gone in just a moment, and you'll forget all about us."

But the woman couldn't stop crying as she dropped her purse into the sack.

"I'm sorry," mumbled Patrick over and over.

"Are we finished yet?" asked Billy as they came to the last man in the lineup. The man emptied his pockets, and Burke danced around the scene, chuckling nervously.

"That's it!" he announced. "Let's be off."

"Well, then," said Hookey, "everybody back aboard!"

The passengers lost no time climbing back into their stagecoach, but the driver paused and looked down at Becky and Patrick.

"Let the children come with us," he said.

For a moment Hookey seemed to think about it, and he pulled at his beard with his two fingers.

"We don't want 'em, Hookey," urged Wendell. "They're more trouble than they're worth. Let 'em go."

"Well . . ." Hookey looked around uncertainly.

"Let them go?" asked Burke, coming around from the other side of the coach. "Absolutely out of the question."

"Why not?" asked Wendell.

"They know about the meeting place." Burke counted off the reasons on his fingers. "They can be made to work, as you see, and they may be useful in the future for bargaining."

Patrick closed his eyes, all hope dashed for escaping Burke and the bushrangers.

"Hmm," Hookey considered. "Well, you heard the man. You and your sister go help with the mail."

A sour-faced Jim prodded Patrick and Becky over to the far side of the road, where Charlie was pulling out mail, slitting it open with his knife, and setting aside the money and checks.

"Oh, and by the way," Hookey asked the coach driver as if he were casually asking for directions, "you didn't happen upon a large, redheaded Irishman out in the bush country, did you? We're searching for him, you see."

The driver only shook his head. "The only ones we've come across are yellow bushrangers."

"Ha! Yellow?" crowed Hookey. "When you make the next town, you can tell everybody how well you were treated by these bushrangers. Now, be on your way."

The horses sprinted and tugged while the driver shouted for them to go faster, and they were gone. It started to drizzle again.

"Mind you keep those letters out of the rain!" ordered Hookey. "Sit under the tree over there so you don't ruin the addresses on the envelopes. And count it up as you go."

Charlie pulled more checks out of the mail and stuffed their leather bag. "A hundred eighty," he counted, pulling out another bill. "Two hundred . . ."

"We should be able to cash some of those," said Billy, watching the counting.

"Can't you count any faster than that, Charlie?" Hookey wondered.

"Two hundred fifty," continued Charlie, ignoring the comments. "Two hundred seventy-five pounds, Hookey."

Hookey brought his horse around and slid up into place on the saddle. "Not bad at all. Put it in the bag, and we'll take a look at it when we get back to camp. And, Billy," he turned to his brother, "take a few pounds with you to fetch some food for us, will you? We can afford to buy this time. Find a farmer or something."

Billy grinned and ran to his horse. "Roast lamb tonight! I know where there's a farm. Be waiting for you back at the camp." A moment later he galloped away.

Hookey was about to turn away when he noticed something about Patrick.

"Hey, what's that?" he asked, leaning closer. Patrick tried to step away.

"No, let me see what's around your neck. I hadn't noticed that before."

Becky stepped between the horse and Patrick. "It's nothing," she began, but Jim only pulled her away and held Patrick from escaping.

"I wouldn't say that," said Hookey. With one hand on the saddle, he leaned down with his hook hand and grabbed Patrick's shirt, then caught the string that held his grandmother's ring and yanked it straight up and off. The string caught Patrick's ears.

"Ow!" cried Patrick. He tried to hold on to the ring but wasn't quick enough.

"I thought I saw something shiny around your neck," Hookey

said, holding the ring up to his eye. "Where did you steal this?"

"You can't have that," replied Patrick. "It belonged to my grandmother." When he reached back up to snatch it back, Jim held his arms.

"Grandma's ring. Even better." Hookey smiled and bit into the ring. "Real gold. Family heirloom. A little plain, maybe, but it'll do." He took off his hat, slipped the ring around his own neck, and laughed. "Thank you so much for giving it to me."

Patrick kicked furiously at Jim's shin behind him.

"You . . ." groaned Jim. Patrick slashed with his elbows and jumped for the horse.

"Get him!" ordered Hookey, reeling back with the frightened horse.

"Give it back!" yelled Patrick. "You're not taking my grandmother's ring."

Hookey held tightly to his horse, like a cowboy on a bucking bronco, but when Patrick grabbed his ankle, he fell halfway off the saddle. The horse continued bucking, and as it ran Patrick dragged through the mud.

"Let go, you lunatic!" cried Hookey, trying desperately to shake free of Patrick's hold.

"Not until"—Patrick gritted his teeth—". . . you give me back . . . my grandmother's ring."

Patrick nearly lost his shoes in the mud, but still he held on while the horse circled wildly. Finally the animal came down on its front two legs, jarring Patrick loose with a vicious shake. At the same time, he heard the explosion of gunfire.

CHAPTER 17

FORCED MARCH

"Oh!" Patrick grunted and rolled as he hit a gravelly, hard patch of roadway, then struggled to his feet. Hookey must have pulled himself back into the saddle, because a moment later Patrick looked up to see the man's blazing black eyes and the end of Hookey's pistol pointed in his face.

"Stubborn little boy, aren't you?" Hookey's finger twitched on the trigger.

Patrick's knees quivered and buckled, and though he commanded his legs not to, they folded underneath him and he fell to his knees.

"That's better." Hookey tucked the ring under his shirt and turned to the others. "Jim, you take him with you on your horse. And mind he doesn't pull you off."

"But he's all muddy, Hookey," protested the other man.

"Do it!" barked Hookey. "And give me the bag."

"I'll take care of it, Hookey." Jim clutched the leather pouch with all the valuables, but Hookey hadn't finished with his gun.

"I won't be saying this again, mate," said Hookey, this time pointing his gun at Jim. "I'm the only one who holds on to the money, understand? Now, give it to me and take care of the kid."

Without another word Jim threw the heavy leather saddlebag at Hookey, who caught it neatly. Jim wheeled his horse around with a vicious jerk on the reins, hauled Patrick up by the back of his shirt, and dropped him on the back of his horse.

"Hold on, boy," he said gruffly, and somehow Patrick did. They galloped past the tree where the men had carefully hung three bags of mail for the next stage to pick up, then disappeared with the others back into the trees in the direction of the bushranger camp.

Riding the way they came, the bushrangers took turns whooping and carrying on, once in a while shooting their guns at birds overhead. Clearly, they didn't care if anyone heard them, and they took their time on the trail. Hookey was quieter than the others, clutching the leather saddlebag with the valuables carefully under his arm.

"What about the kids now?" asked Jim. "It worked once for them to stop the stagecoach, but it won't work again."

"He's right," agreed Charlie. "The trick is over. Now all the coach drivers will know. And what if someone is out looking for them?"

"Ah, they wouldn't know where to start," replied Hookey glumly. "We'll decide back at the camp what to do."

Patrick knew Becky was keeping an eye on him from the back of Charlie's horse, but Patrick was too tired even to nod or wave at her. He closed his eyes and listened to the men argue about the money, about their next robbery, about finding his father. *I wonder how Michael is doing*, he thought. *Ma probably hasn't let him out of her sight since Becky and I disappeared*.

As they approached the entrance to Kangaroo Springs, he thought he heard the kookaburra's laugh once more, only this one sounded a little different.

Actually, something sounded *very* different about the kookaburra laughing softly in the trees above the trees that guarded the entrance to Kangaroo Springs. When Patrick looked up into the dripping trees, he stared straight at the wide-eyed face of Jack Duggan, perched in an upper branch!

I'm seeing things, decided Patrick, trying not to fall off the back of the horse. Just behind him, it didn't look as if Becky or anyone else had noticed. But there it was again—Jack Duggan's kooka-burra call!

If Jack is here, thought Patrick, *he's not alone.*

When they arrived at the empty camp, Patrick slipped off the horse and tumbled to the ground while Jim kept a close watch over him and his sister. Wendell and Hookey swung off their own horses, arguing fiercely.

"I still say we should have let 'em go back at the stage road," said Wendell, tying up his horse. "Who's going to feed them? Not Your Majesty, Sir Hookey Simpson. All you do is wave your pistol around and watch us jump."

"You ungrateful little wombat . . ." began Hookey, dropping the reins to face Wendell.

"All right, boys." Burke stepped between the warring bushrangers. "I'm not paying you to fight each other. And I'm growing hungry."

"Yeh." Wendell dropped his fists. "So what's taking Billy so long? He said he would be here before us with all the food."

Burke frowned and looked around the camp. "He's a fast rider. He should have been here by now. Charlie, you know where he went. Ride back quick and see what's taking him so long."

Charlie grinned. "If I know Billy, he's probably sitting under a tree and helping himself to a good meal. That's what'll be taking him—"

"All right," interrupted Hookey. "Just go find him and bring back the dinner. Jim, you start a fire. I'll keep an eye on these kids."

Over the next hour Jim only succeeded in making a lot of smoke, and Wendell was left to recount their loot. Burke tried to follow Hookey around as the bushranger's leader paced the camp with a gun in his hand.

"How long are we simply going to sit here?" asked Burke. "We've already lost too much time."

"Listen, Mr. Burke." Hookey stopped his pacing. "I told you we'll find your Irishman. We'll go out after we get a fire started and something in our bellies."

Burke put out his hands. "I was merely asking."

"Yeh, well, sometimes . . ." Hookey frowned and didn't finish.

"I can't get this fire started," grumbled Jim. "It's too wet."

Patrick listened for the kookaburra call again but heard nothing except the steady drip of the rain in the trees.

"What do you see out there?" asked Jim as he tried to shelter his damp pile of sticks and leaves. It did no good.

"Me?" asked Patrick, looking back to the camp. "Nothing."

If only I had a chance to tell Becky, he thought.

"Yeh, sure." Jim lit another match, but it went out, and he threw it down in disgust. "Hey, could somebody do something about these two kids? They're making me nervous."

"We'll help with the fire," volunteered Becky.

"Oh, so you think *you* can get something started?"

"I think so." Becky sounded sure of herself.

"Well, go ahead and try, young lady. I'd like to see this."

Becky and Patrick tried their best to find a dry bunch of twigs, but they had no better luck than the bushranger.

"We almost have it." Patrick bent down next to the twigs and blew until he felt dizzy while Becky cupped her hands over the spark.

"I saw Jack Duggan in the trees," he whispered.

"What did you say?" Becky looked at him, puzzled.

"Here, you need something that isn't wet," said Hookey, glancing around the camp. "Wendell, you have anything dry in your saddlebags over there?" He reached into the other man's leather bags and smiled when he pulled out a handful of papers that looked like a wrinkled book. "Well, what have we here? Something you wanted to read, Wendell?"

Wendell, who was still counting coins and gold watches, paled when he saw what Hookey held up.

"You never told us you were interested in the Bible, Wendell, my boy." Hookey waved the pages in the air. "This is the Bible I ripped up and threw out back at the cabin, isn't it?"

"What if it is?" Wendell continued counting the gold.

Becky glanced over at her brother, but he could only return her puzzled look. *Why would Wendell have done that? Why would he have saved the book?*

"Well, it's a good thing you did." Hookey seemed to answer Patrick's silent question. "Because it looks like this is going to be good for something after all."

Hookey tossed the two halves of the Bible over to Becky, who tried to catch them and smooth out a couple of ripped pages.

"What was that verse you preached at me, girl?" Hookey leaned over to taunt Becky while Burke watched with interest. "Something about me breaking my arms?"

" 'A little that a righteous man hath is better than the riches of many wicked,' " she recited quietly, and only Patrick could hear her words. " 'For the arms of the wicked shall be broken.' "

"What's that, young lady?" Hookey put his hand to his ear. "Speak up so your Irish friend can hear. He missed your lovely sermon when we were back at your home."

Becky knelt by the cold fire pit and lovingly put the two halves of the Bible together, ignoring the man's words. A few of the pages were wrinkled and torn, and the cover was dirty, but it was all there.

"I said, speak up!"

"Come on, Hookey," said Wendell quietly. "We don't have time for that."

Hookey spun on his heel and glared at his brother-in-law. "Oh, so now it's Wendell to the rescue again, is it? Wendell saved the holy book, and now he's going to save the holy kids!"

"That's not it." Wendell tried to defend himself, but Hookey only cackled with delight.

"Fire starter," he whooped, turning back to Becky. "Use your book to start the fire, preacher-girl."

Becky didn't move.

"Do it now!" he bellowed. "I want to see a fire so we can cook our dinner. You want to eat, don't you?"

"I won't use the Bible to start the fire, Mr. Hookey." Becky stood up. "I don't care what you say."

"Well, aren't you the stubborn little preacher-girl." Hookey sniffed and rubbed his nose while he nervously twirled the gun in his hand. He looked around the camp, and Patrick returned to his pile of twigs, blowing furiously at a spark. Suddenly one of them caught fire, sending up a brave yellow flame.

"I've got it!" said Patrick, fanning the flames carefully.

Hookey took one look at the fire and frowned, and they all waited quietly as the flames crackled, popped, and grew larger.

"Well, looks like you got lucky, boy," Hookey finally admitted. Without warning he stepped over to the fire and snuffed it out with his boot. "But I still think your book will make a good fire starter. Try again."

Becky gasped and stared down at the smoldering branches. Patrick closed his eyes and leaned back on his heels.

I tried my best, God, Patrick prayed silently.

Hookey hooted with amusement.

"Aw, Hookey," Wendell protested once more. "All we needed was a fire, and there we had one."

"Keep it to yourself!" Hookey thundered as he pulled out his gun again and waved it at everyone in the camp. "Between Wendell's whimpering and these two fool kids, I believe I'm going crazy."

"Graham . . ." Burke stepped slowly forward and put out his hand.

"Only my mother calls me Graham!"

"Of course—"

"Listen, I already said we'd find your Irishman. But something's not right here. First my brother disappears, and now . . ."

His voice trailed off as Charlie's horse returned to the camp, minus Charlie.

CHAPTER 18

CAPTIVE AT KANGAROO SPRINGS

"There's an explanation for everything," said Burke, checking Charlie's empty saddle, as if the thin man might be hiding on it somewhere. "He probably found Billy, and then his horse somehow got away from him."

Hookey took a deep breath and finally lowered his gun. "Maybe. But I've never known him to do something that stupid. Jim, Wendell, I want you to go see what's going on. If you're not back in two hours, we're leaving. Understand?"

While the men argued, Patrick and Becky worked on getting the fire started again after Becky had carefully tucked the Bible back into Wendell's saddlebags. Everyone stopped to listen when Jim and Wendell jumped on their horses and thundered out of the gully.

At first all they heard were the echoes of Wendell whistling at his horse and the dull patter of hooves.

"There!" said Hookey after a few minutes of silence. "Did you hear that, Burke?"

Burke stood still, frowned, and shook his head. "Might have been a shout. I don't know."

Patrick was sure he heard something, too, only it was hard to tell just what. A shout, or a shot? The gully seemed to take every sound—especially from the direction of the entrance—and twist it around. And there was the laugh again!

149

"Ah, just a bird." Burke dismissed the sounds with a wave of his hand. "Sounds like your kooka-borrow bird."

"Right." Hookey didn't look convinced, but he turned back to the fire. Only this time he didn't have as long to wait before two riderless horses came trotting back to the camp.

"That's it, Hookey." Burke looked around the camp with wild eyes. "We're getting out of here. Somebody's pulling your men off their horses."

Hookey grabbed one of the animals' reins.

"Tie the children's wrists and put them on the horses," yelped Burke. He scanned the growing shadows around him. "Backward."

"What? I say leave them here."

For once Patrick agreed with Hookey, but Burke shook his head.

"They're still useful to us. If there are troopers out there, we could use a couple of good shields."

Hookey smiled slightly as he understood what Burke was telling him. Patrick wondered if they should take a chance on running.

Becky gave him a warning look. "We'll get out of this," she promised softly. "Let's just do what they tell us."

Burke hurried to tie Patrick's and Becky's wrists again, and they were each hoisted up into a saddle. Next, Hookey strung the reins of the two horses together so that they could lead them single file between Burke's horse in the lead and Hookey's in the rear. Patrick sat facing the rear of his horse, looking straight at Becky's back and holding on desperately with his bound wrists to keep from sliding off.

"Hey, do you hear me?" Hookey cupped his bad hand to his mouth and shouted into the woods, still holding the moneybag under his other arm. "If you can't see, I've got a rifle pointed at these two kids, here, and I'm not afraid to use it."

No one replied, and Hookey's words echoed throughout the gully.

"You back away now!" Hookey kept his rifle ready. "Anything happens to us, and you won't be speaking to these kids again. Hear me?"

Patrick held on tightly to the saddle as they slowly bounced down the trail that led out of Kangaroo Springs. Somewhere in the trees Jack's kookaburra laughed again.

"What was that?" asked Hookey.

Patrick knew he might not get another chance. In the split second the bushranger was looking up at the trees, he slapped his horse as hard as he could with both hands and tumbled off the end, right in front of Becky's frightened horse.

He heard a shot and Hookey's shout. The horses reared up in fright. In the confusion Becky nearly fell on top of Patrick.

"Patrick!" cried Becky as she crawled after him through the trees. There was no time to untie their wrists, and Patrick could only drag his own rope behind him.

"This way," he told her. She was two, maybe three, steps behind him.

"You two!" hollered Hookey. He had tumbled off his horse, too, but began shooting wildly in their direction.

Which way? Patrick thought desperately. He wondered where Jack was, where Burke was, and who else might be around. But there was no time to look.

"Stay down," said Patrick as they scrambled from tree to tree.

"You're not getting away," Hookey roared just behind them. "Stop now and I won't hurt you."

Halfway up the slope the surrounding hills and trees abruptly thinned out into a grassy meadow. They had no choice but to run into the open on their way to the top of the hill. Patrick glanced at his sister.

"We'll make it," he told her. "You said so yourself."

Becky nodded. "To the top of this little hill. Run!"

Patrick was afraid to look back, but they had a good head start into the meadow when Hookey yelled at them again.

"Far enough," he cried, firing twice. It sounded closer than Patrick had hoped.

"Oh!" Becky groaned, and when Patrick looked back, she was on her face in the meadow, not moving. Patrick's pounding heart felt as though it had stopped.

"Becky!" he cried out, but for a moment he could not make his feet move. Hookey was closer and walked slowly up to her body.

It can't be! All Patrick's strength drained away when he saw Becky lying on the ground. Even from five feet away, he could tell she wasn't moving, not even a little bit. As Hookey climbed up to look at his kill, Patrick just dropped to his knees, tore off the ropes from his wrists, and cried.

"I told you kids not to do that." Hookey looked down at his victim and poked at her side gently with the toe of his boot. He held his handgun loosely at his side, and his saddlebag with the robbery loot was draped over his shoulder like a prize. "Look, it wasn't my fault. . . ."

From somewhere down the hill, Patrick thought he heard other voices. But before he knew what had happened, Becky sprang to life like a snake striking at its prey. She grabbed Hookey's leg and they both tumbled down the hill.

"The gun!" she cried. "Get the gun, Patrick!"

It took a moment to realize what was happening, and another to realize that other people were charging at the wrestling match. There was Jack Duggan, running up at them. Behind him was Jack's father, then someone else. The Old Man!

"Patrick!" Becky yelled once more as Hookey roared like a bear. They fell and rolled again, and his hand waved wildly.

It was all the invitation Patrick needed. He jumped to his feet, took three giant steps, and launched himself in a flying leap at the hand with the gun.

The weapon went off harmlessly, but Patrick was so intent on squeezing it from Hookey's hand that nothing would have made a difference.

"Let go of my sister!" he screamed and sat on the man's arm while Becky shouted and pounded on Hookey's chest with her two fists. Something snapped loudly beneath him, and Hookey howled with pain while the gun dropped in Patrick's lap.

"My wrist," groaned the man, and he rolled over on the ground. "Oh, my wrist."

By that time the others had joined in, and Jack and his father easily held Hookey down. Patrick felt strong hands on his shoulders, pulling him off gently but firmly. He looked up into the face of the Old Man.

"You don't know how glad I am to see you." Patrick wrapped his arms around the man, who chuckled and finally held Patrick at arm's length.

"Look at you. You look like some kind of dirty bushman. Your clothes torn to shreds, filthy as a wombat, hair looks like a kookaburra nest."

"He's the kookaburra." Patrick smiled and pointed at Jack. "Or one of them."

"Get off me!" groaned Hookey, but no one paid attention.

"You heard the bird calls?" Jack beamed. "I wasn't sure."

"Never mind that," said the Old Man. "Are you all right, Becky?"

Jack and his father continued to hold Hookey down while Becky rose to her feet. She smoothed out her matted hair and dirty clothes and looked down as if realizing for the first time how terrible she looked.

"I'm all right." She managed to choke out the words. "I *think* I'm all right." She looked up shyly at her brother, who looked no better, but the smile in her eyes said everything.

"I told you we'd make it." Patrick smiled back. "You were great, Becky, grabbing his leg like that."

"So were you, little brother."

"Ow!" Hookey screamed again.

"What did you do to him?" wondered the Old Man, holding Patrick around the shoulder. They took a step back from the groaning bushranger.

"Broke my wrist!" howled Hookey.

"Sorry about that." Jack grinned like a cowboy who had just roped another calf in a rodeo. "That's the last one, Pa."

Mr. Duggan nodded proudly at his son. "Good job, Jack. Let's tie him up, just like we did all the other fellows."

"What about Burke?" Patrick looked around.

"We got all of 'em," Jack reassured him.

This time Patrick let himself smile in relief, but he worried again when he looked at the bushranger. *I really didn't mean to*, he thought, and he winced every time Hookey cried out in pain.

"Not exactly an intelligent bunch." Mr. Duggan clapped his hands. "We sprung on 'em with a rope each time they'd come riding out of that tunnel between the trees. They were just blinkin' their eyes like rats in a trap."

"We were sure ready for you, too," added Jack. "Sitting here by the entrance all morning. Where'd you go?"

"We'll have time for stories later, Jack," his father warned him.

"But where are they now?" wondered Becky.

"Really, don't worry." Jack gave Hookey's rope a tug. "We loaded them into the back of the wagon, down by the path near the creek. Constable Fitzgerald's eyes are going to pop out when we come rolling back into town with the Hookey Simpson Gang."

"But Burke . . ." Becky still looked worried.

Hookey only moaned with pain, and Jack kept an eye on his man as they led him down the hill. This time it was the bushranger's turn to wear a rope handcuff. His shirt was ripped down the front.

"And what about all their guns?" Patrick noticed the men weren't carrying any.

"We threw every last one of their guns into the stream," sniffed the Old Man, "where we should've thrown the lot of these bushrangers." He took up a position next to Hookey.

"Patrick." Becky pointed down at the pistol Patrick was still clutching.

"Where did that come from?" Patrick looked at the gun for the first time and felt almost sick to his stomach at the touch of the weapon. Without thinking, he leaned back and threw it as far as he could into the bush.

"Hey," protested Hookey. "I had to play a whole night of cards for that pistol. Won it fair and legal."

Jack held on to the rope as they stepped down around the entrance into Kangaroo Springs. "Where you're going, mister, you're not going to be needing anything like that."

"Wait a minute." The Old Man held up his hand, and they all

stopped as he looked more closely at the ring Hookey still wore around his neck.

"That's—" Patrick began, but his sister hushed him. The Old Man reached out and took their grandmother's ring off Hookey's neck, cradling it in his hand.

"Doesn't belong to you, does it, mister?" The Old Man looked at the ring for a moment with a faraway look in his eyes. He didn't seem to expect an answer. "Belonged to my wife, as a matter of fact."

"We tied up our horses right back there," explained Mr. Duggan, not realizing what the Old Man was saying. With everything happening so fast, Patrick wasn't sure, either, and he stared as the bearded man pressed the ring back into Patrick's hand.

"There you go." He turned to leave.

"Wait a minute." Patrick planted his feet. "You can't just say something like that and walk away. That ring belonged to my grandmother. . . ."

The Old Man stopped after a couple of steps, took a deep breath, and turned around slowly.

"So it did."

"But we're not both right," Patrick told the Old Man. "If we were, you would have to be my grandfather."

When the Old Man looked straight into Patrick's eyes, Patrick saw himself for an instant.

"So I am."

"I don't understand." Patrick's head spun while a slow grin spread across Becky's face. "I thought your name was Hughes. Adam Hughes. That's the name on the certificate in your boat."

"The certificate," the Old Man repeated with a chuckle as they walked again toward where the horses were tied up. "You know where I got that certificate?"

"For being a paddle-steamer captain?" guessed Becky.

The Old Man shook his head.

"You mean you're not really a captain?" Patrick couldn't believe what he was hearing.

"Of course I am. Know the river better than anyone else alive.

It's just that, well, that certificate helped me get a job once. . . ." He swallowed hard. "I haven't told this to anyone else."

"Who are you, really?" Patrick finally asked, his voice quiet. But by that time he already knew. He just wanted to hear it with his own ears.

"It's been almost thirty years since they took me from Ireland for stealing," said the Old Man, looking straight ahead. "Sent me here to Australia when your pa was about the same age you are now."

"But you just disappeared," said Patrick. His mouth felt dry.

The Old Man shrugged. "At first I thought my family was better off without me. Me, a convict. Then when I learned Elisabeth had died—that would be your grandmother—I don't know, I suppose something just kind of shut down inside."

"But you still had your children in Ireland who needed you." Becky took hold of his arm as they walked, and he smiled weakly.

"You couldn't tell me that at the time. I never figured a convict was much use as a father. Guess I didn't figure I was much use as anything until I met Adam."

"Adam Hughes?" asked Patrick. The name on the certificate in the wheelhouse.

"Adam Hughes," repeated the Old Man. By that time they were back under the trees. "Nephew of the owner at the sheep station where I worked—prison work. I don't know how, but we became friends. And I served my time."

"What happened to him?" asked Becky.

"He went back home to Boston, taking a job on a clipper ship, and he kindly let me take over his name. Not so proud to say so, but it got me my first job on the river."

Mr. Duggan had been listening but still seemed confused. "So you're not really Hughes?"

"To you, sir, I'm still who I've called myself for the past twenty years, working on the Murray River, and I'll thank you for keeping this little secret just between you and me."

Mr. Duggan's eyes were wide with surprise, but he nodded seriously, and he helped walk their prisoner more quickly. Jack had trotted on ahead and hadn't heard anything.

"And you two," the Old Man continued, stopping for a moment and putting his hands on Becky's and Patrick's shoulders. "I'm sorry for deceiving you. All this time I've pretended . . ."

"That's all right." Patrick didn't know what else to say.

"Ma is going to scream!" Becky bubbled.

"I knew who you were the first time I saw you, Patrick," continued the Old Man. "As soon as I saw Elisabeth's ring on your neck that day when you first walked onto my paddle steamer." He smiled sadly. "I gave it to her back in 1823."

"And all this time you pretended not to know us?"

"I suppose I just didn't know how to step back into the family," the Old Man went on at last. His eyes were glistening. "I'm sorry for misleading you. I was a bitter old man after all those years. . . ."

"But what do we call you now?" Becky wanted to know. "Grandfather?"

The Old Man stopped for a moment and thought. "Captain is fine for now. I'm not sure how soon I'll get used to being a grandfather."

They all laughed, and Patrick had to repeat the word.

"Grandfather." Patrick pulled the ring out of his pocket and pushed it into his grandfather's big hand. "Captain Grandfather, you should have this back. This belongs to you."

"But there are still so many things you have to explain to us." Becky shook her head in amazement.

"And now you can really help us find Pa."

"Captain!" yelled Jack, running toward them. His face was red with excitement. "The bushrangers are gone. And so are all our horses!"

CHAPTER 19

LONG WAY TO ECHUCA

"What?" the Old Man thundered and ran the rest of the way back to where they had left their wagon. "What do you mean, gone?"

But his question was already answered. Mr. Duggan's wagon was tipped rudely over on its side, and the horses had been unhitched.

"How did they all get loose?" Patrick wondered. "Didn't you say . . ."

"We tied them up good," insisted Jack, shaking his head.

The only one smiling was Hookey, and he looked around at the trees, as if the others were hiding.

"You couldn't tie up my mates and get away with it. Now they're going to come get me, and I don't know if I'm going to be able to hold them back from—"

"Quiet, you." Mr. Duggan stepped up to Hookey, but the Old Man stopped him.

"Brave man." Hookey taunted him. "Why don't you take these ropes off and say that again?"

"Yeh, my pa will break your other arm," replied Jack.

"All right, that's enough," warned the Old Man. "We just need to get out of here quickly."

"You can't outride my boys without horses." Hookey looked smug.

"I don't understand how they got themselves loose." Jack held up a couple of the ropes he had used to tie the bushrangers in his wagon. Several looked as if they had been sliced in half.

"I knew it!" Becky gasped and looked around nervously. "They didn't get loose by themselves."

"They had help," added Patrick, catching on to what his sister was saying. "Burke. He must have slipped away, then came back and untied everyone."

"Good man, Burke." Hookey grinned, and Mr. Duggan looked as if he would hit him in the nose.

"Which means they're out there." Jack started looking around, too. "Five of them, and five of us. At least they don't have any guns, either."

"Burke does," Becky reminded him.

"Hey, Billy!" Hookey shouted. "You can come out now!"

Mr. Duggan held the prisoner's arms even more tightly, bringing a howl of pain.

"I told you to be quiet!" he ordered.

"That's enough, Claude." The Old Man sounded stern. "We're not going to start treating them the way they treated the children. But we're going to deliver this bushranger up to Constable Fitzgerald if I have to drag him all the way back to Echuca on foot."

"No need for that," said Patrick as he spied something moving in a distant grove of trees. "Looks like one of your horses over there."

"Good!" The Old Man pointed at the horse, and Jack ran to investigate. "Hurry, now. They might be coming back any minute. Becky, Patrick, let's get this wagon right side up."

Ten minutes later they had managed to round up Mr. Duggan's other horse and right the wagon. Becky even found the Old Man's horse.

"Dirty bushrangers," mumbled Mr. Duggan as he tried to line up his horse team. "Sliced up a perfectly good harness."

"Make it work," commanded the Old Man, climbing onto the back of his own horse. "But let's start moving."

Only minutes later they were crashing through the bush over two ruts, barely a trail. Mr. Duggan shouted and whistled at his horses as if they were in a race for their lives.

"Yah!" He slapped with the reins.

"Won't do you any good to run," Hookey mumbled as they hit an especially bumpy stretch of trail. He wiggled and tested the ropes that tied him at the ankles and the wrists. "My boys will be here real soon."

Patrick tried not to look at their prisoner, but of course they all had to sit in the back of the wagon together. He held on tightly and watched his "new" grandfather riding ahead of them.

"Maybe they went off to get some new guns," Patrick wondered aloud. In his mind he could imagine the rest of the Simpson Gang thundering down the trail, guns blazing, coming to rescue their leader.

No one disagreed as they continued on.

After a while the Old Man held up his hand and mopped his brow. "Rest here for a minute. It's been three hours since we started out. Be dark soon."

And still no bushrangers, Patrick worried.

"Maybe we should have kept their guns for ourselves," suggested Mr. Duggan.

"No, Claude." The Old Man shook his head. "I promised the children's mother there would be none of that."

"And who needs guns?" Jack jumped out to stretch his legs. He twirled the loop of one of his ropes like a circus performer.

"I need a drink," demanded Hookey.

While Mr. Duggan, Hookey, and Jack got a drink down closer to the stream, Patrick and Becky kept a nervous watch with the Old Man.

"Just between you and me, kids, I can't imagine why the rest of the gang hasn't showed up yet to reclaim their leader." The Old Man rested in his saddle, took a sip from his canteen, and passed it to them.

"And to come get their money," added Patrick, pointing at the leather saddlebag in the front of the wagon.

"The money!" said Becky. "I have an idea. Patrick, hand me Mr. Duggan's bag."

Patrick was sitting on Mr. Duggan's worn canvas bag; he picked it up and held it out.

"Hold it open," she told him. "Hurry!"

She emptied all the money and watches from Hookey's sack into it.

"Why are we doing this?" asked Patrick.

"Never mind," she answered, checking to make sure Hookey didn't see them. "Just find a few rocks and leaves and put them in there, instead."

The Old Man seemed to understand her perfectly.

"Oh, I see." Patrick grinned and did as his sister told him. No one said anything when the others returned from the stream, except the Old Man whispered something into Mr. Duggan's ear as he handed him his bag. They both grinned as Mr. Duggan took the reins again.

"So where's your gang, Mr. Simpson?" Jack asked. "Looks like they're not going to show after all."

Hookey's eyes were closed in pain, and his voice sounded more distant than ever. "They'll be along. You watch."

Patrick and Becky watched as they continued on, but the closer they came to the place where the creek joined the Murray, the more he wondered why the bushranger gang hadn't shown up to claim Hookey. Mr. Duggan wasn't slowing down, either.

"We're almost there," reported the Old Man only moments before Mr. Duggan stopped the wagon with a jerk.

"What's going on?" Hookey opened his eyes.

A single shot told him what he wanted to know, and a smile spread across Hookey's face when he saw what Patrick had already seen.

"Once again, what an astonishing coincidence," said Conrad

Burke. He looked at his pistol as if it were the first time he had ever used it, and his black horse sidestepped nervously in front of them on the trail. "I thought perhaps I'd find you coming this way."

CHAPTER 20

ONE STEP AHEAD

"About time you caught up with us." Hookey tried to straighten up, but Jack had tied his ropes too tightly. "Get me untied, Burke."

Strangely, Burke ignored Hookey, but he kept an eye on the Old Man.

"Off the horse," he ordered, and the Old Man had no choice. "Drop your weapons on the ground."

The Old Man held up his hand. "No weapons here."

"That's Burke," Patrick whispered to Mr. Duggan, who nodded as if he had already figured it out.

"Oh, pardon me," said Burke with a large smile once the Old Man was off his horse and standing next to the wagon. "Conrad Burke, at your service. But first, that leather satchel, if you don't mind."

Jack hesitated for only a moment before grabbing the bushrangers' leather sack and tossing it at the horseman. Burke caught it in midair, felt the weight with his hand, and tucked it under his arm.

"Thank you so much." He grinned again and adjusted his hat. "I hadn't realized this sort of thing could be so pleasant."

"Enough with the Irish gentleman act!" fumed Hookey from the back of the wagon. "Get me out of here, Burke!"

Burke looked puzzled and turned his head to the side. "Odd, but do you hear something?"

Patrick couldn't believe what he was seeing, and apparently, neither could Hookey.

"Burke!" shouted Hookey. "I said, get . . . me . . . untied."

Burke guided his horse slowly around to the side of the wagon and looked down at Hookey, who could only squirm like a furious inchworm. Becky and Patrick did their best to stay as far away from him as they could.

"Why, look who else is here," continued Burke. "Mr. Simpson, I do believe you've gotten yourself into a bind. Or how do you Aussies put it? You're up a gum tree?" Burke laughed.

"This isn't a bit funny, Burke." Hookey sputtered and fumed. "Are you going to quit talking and untie me, or what?"

Burke sighed. "Regrettably, no. You've proven yourself to be a bit of a bumbler, I'm afraid. I don't need you anymore."

"What are you talking about?" Hookey exploded. "You need me to find your prisoner. I'm the only one—"

"Ah, but that's where you're wrong, my friend. I have a very clear idea now where to look. And your associates have agreed to work for considerably less than what you have been demanding."

Mr. Duggan spoke up for the first time. "Where are the others? Where's your gang?"

"My mates will be here any minute." Hookey looked sure of himself.

Burke just smiled. "Ah yes. The others. I'm afraid I cannot divulge their whereabouts, but I can assure you they'll not be joining us. They are, after all, in mourning."

"Mourning?" asked the Old Man. "What are you talking about?"

"Yes, it was touching to see," replied Burke, pointing his pistol at Hookey. "Even tough old Jim was moved almost to tears to hear how Hookey here was killed back at Kangaroo Springs and his body taken away. He heard the shot. And your younger brother Billy, well, he was positively devastated by the news."

Hookey's eyes narrowed as he finally understood what Burke was saying. "Is that what you told them? You, you . . ."

"Oh dear." Burke held up his hand. "No need to thank me. You might like to know that your friends really did desire to come along and try to recover your body. I convinced them, however, that since I was the only one left with a gun, I should ride up and see what I could accomplish. So when I return with the money, well, they'll just naturally have to accept their new temporary leader. How does the 'Burke Gang' sound to you?"

"You're crazy if you think you can pull this off," sputtered Hookey. His eyes nearly popped, and his face was crimson with rage.

"Ah." Burke smiled, backing away. "But I already have. And by the time your friends hear you're really not dead, I will have located the missing convict. That done, I can easily move on to San Francisco with a nice sum of retirement money."

Patrick tried not to look at his sister, and she put a hand on his arm.

Just don't look in the bag, Burke, he thought.

"I'll pass along your greetings to your father, my young friends, when I see him." Burke tipped his hat as he rode off. "I expect that will be quite soon."

"Burke!" screamed Hookey. "You can't do this!"

But Conrad Burke only disappeared back into the bush, laughing.

The Old Man wasted no time remounting his horse.

"What's your hurry?" asked Jack. "You heard what he said about the others. Nobody's coming after us."

"Check your father's bag," Becky whispered as she found a better seat, as far away from Hookey as she could manage.

"Oh, dear . . ." Jack's voice trailed off when he peeked inside the canvas sack.

"He'll be back," said Mr. Duggan, urging his horse on. "After he checks *his* bag."

The rest of the ride was a blur in Patrick's mind. He and Becky both tried to stay away from Hookey as they jolted down the trail. As it turned out, he didn't have to worry. The man said nothing, only scowled into the moonlight behind them. Hookey worked his jaw up and down as if he were chewing something or silently scolding someone. And any minute Patrick expected to see Burke returning for his stolen loot and twice as angry at having been fooled. Thinking about his new grandfather, Patrick nodded off to a restless sleep.

"Almost home," reported Jack a few minutes later. "The Old Man's place is just around the bend there."

Patrick jerked his bobbing head awake. His neck felt stiff and sore. He noticed, too, that he had been drooling on his shirt and quickly looked around to see if anyone else had seen him. No, too dark. In the distance he thought he could see a faint light where the cabin should be, and his stomach rumbled with hunger.

"What if Burke returns?" Patrick asked.

"I don't know, Patrick," Becky replied, checking their progress. A few stars sparkled on the river that lay to their right. "If he hasn't caught up to us by now, I don't know. But listen . . ."

Patrick strained to hear a low whistle, then a faint shout, then a bark.

"Dogs!" Patrick got up on his knees, and a minute later they were surrounded by eager brown hound dogs and a dozen men on horseback, the men from Echuca. Most had lanterns, and the yellow lights danced around them. Mr. Duggan's horses started to rear up.

"Hey, Kenneth, call off your animals!" Mr. Duggan yelled at the lead man on horseback. The dogs seemed to think they were hunting for Patrick and Becky as they circled the wagon with their noses in the air, and set up a new howl.

"We captured Hookey Simpson!" Jack reported excitedly, but no one could hear him over the noise of the dogs.

"That's enough!" the man named Kenneth at last yelled at his pack. Patrick shivered when he remembered him as the leader of the mob in town last Sunday. His dogs weren't listening, though, and continued their loud dance around the wagon.

"Seen him?" cried the man, almost as excited as his animals. He acted as if they should know what he was talking about.

"Hold it, Kenneth," objected the Old Man, raising his voice

above the noise. "Who are you looking for? What's all this?"

"We captured—" Jack tried once more.

"You've been away from town a few days, Old Man," the man named Kenneth interrupted while his dogs leaped in the air around him. "We've almost caught up to that escaped convict. Thought we were catching up to him a few miles away, but the dogs keep losing the scent."

"How do you know it was the convict?" asked Becky, looking interested.

"It's him." The man sounded sure of himself. "A farmer outside of town said a red-haired drifter slept in his barn. That's where we got the scent in the first place. We've been lettin' the dogs out this past week, off and on, and they're catching the scent, sure enough. Constable Fitzgerald says—"

"Hello, who's this?" One of the other men caught sight of their cargo.

"Hookey Simpson," Jack reported proudly. "We captured Hookey Simpson, the bushranger. We're taking him back to town, if you fellows would just get your dogs out of the way."

The men all gathered around and whistled with admiration. Hookey only glared back like a captured animal.

"Why didn't you say so in the first place?" asked their leader. "We'll drag him into town with you."

"I tried to tell you before," said Jack, "but you kept interrupt—"

One of the hounds cut in with a new howl as they gave up on the scents around the wagon and headed off in a new direction.

"Ken!" shouted one of the men. "There they go again!"

Kenneth looked over at them and shrugged as he rode off. Obviously the chase was more exciting than the capture.

"That's the way it's been the last couple of days," said Kenneth. "Here we go again."

Patrick sighed with relief to hear the dogs disappear into the darkness until he remembered who was still riding with them in the wagon.

"Hoo," breathed Mr. Duggan. "I'm glad to be rid of that bunch. Almost as bad as the Hookey Simpson Gang."

Jack laughed. Patrick could only smile and shake his head.

"I sure hope it's mealtime when we get back home." Jack rubbed his hands together. "I'm starving. How about you?"

Patrick looked over at his grandfather. "We've got a little searching of our own to do yet, I think."

"Patrick's right," said the Old Man. "But first we need to take my grandchildren home before we deliver Mr. Simpson up to the constable. They've had quite a time."

Jack looked from Becky and Patrick and back to the Old Man as their wagon rolled under the gum trees. Erin's Landing was just ahead.

"Did you hear him say 'grandchildren,' Pa?"

"Eh? We're all a little tired, Jack."

The Old Man spurred his horse on to lead the way home to Erin's Landing. Patrick could almost smell dinner cooking as he closed his eyes and took a deep breath. *Johnnycakes and sausages*, he thought. *That would be perfect.*

"Ma-aa!"

Patrick nearly jumped out of his seat when he heard the blood-curdling yell from the trail in front of them. He knew in a second who it was, though.

"Ma, come quick! They're back!" screamed Michael.

What's Michael doing out here in the dark? he wondered. Patrick looked ahead of the wagon and sighted the shape of his little brother sprinting down the trail and screaming at the top of his lungs, his koala wrapped around his shoulders.

"Ma! Ma-aa! Coo-EEE!"

Jack chuckled as they pulled up to Erin's Landing. "They're going to hear him all the way back in Echuca."

They could still hear Michael yelling inside, and then a moment later their little brother darted back out the front door, dragging their mother behind him. Her eyes were wide with surprise, and she stood rooted to the front porch, taking it all in.

"Ma!" Becky nearly flew out of the wagon to give her mother a hug, and Patrick wasn't far behind.

"I knew they'd bring you back," whispered their mother

through a fountain of tears. She covered them with flour hand-prints while Michael danced around and Christopher the koala held on for dear life.

"Did you get the bad—" Michael gulped when he noticed who was still tied up in the back of the wagon, but apparently Hookey Simpson had lost his fight. The bushranger only sat still, staring at nothing with an empty, resigned expression.

"Oh my." Mrs. McWaid wiped her eyes on her apron, smearing flour all over her face. "You two have a lot of explaining to do."

"You have two fine children here, Mrs. McWaid," said Mr. Duggan. "They're a bit tired out now, but I wouldn't worry about them for a minute."

"Yes, well, we'll make sure we get them to bed." Their mother was smiling. "But you have no idea what the last few days have been like."

She held Patrick and Becky tightly with both arms. "I know I've said this before, but this time I am definitely not going to let these two out of my sight, maybe for the next ten years."

"Ma . . ." Patrick squirmed a little, but his mother only squeezed more tightly.

"I mean it. Someone's going to have to make up for the fright you've put me through. And, Mr. Duggan, I don't know how to thank you."

He shook his head. "It's not me you should be thanking. The Old Man, there, he's the one who followed the trail to the bush-rangers' hideout. If it was just Jack and me, we'd still be wandering around out there in the bush."

The Old Man remained sitting quietly on his horse behind the wagon, watching the reunion. "But it was young Jack who roped all the bushrangers as they came out," he volunteered. "Never seen anything like it. Not bad for a larrikin."

"Just a little something I learned at a circus." Jack looked at his feet. "Wasn't nothing at all."

Mrs. McWaid smiled. "Well, if you gentlemen will all stop being so modest and come in the house, maybe I can feed you something and hear the whole story."

"I'm sorry, but the bushranger, ma'am." Mr. Duggan nodded in the direction of their prisoner. "We'll need to be taking him into town right away. But another time we'll be sure to tell you the whole story."

Becky broke away from her mother and ran over to the Old Man's horse.

"Just one minute, please?" she asked him. "Before you leave again."

For a moment the Old Man looked tongue-tied, but he let her pull him out of his saddle, then followed her stiffly as she took his arm and led him back to the house.

"Mother," she said seriously, "there's something else you need to know."

"That's right!" added Patrick, almost jumping up and down with excitement. "He's—"

Becky stopped her brother with her hand. "I was telling her, Patrick."

She squeezed the Old Man's arm. "Ma, I'd like you to meet Patrick McWaid. Our grandfather."

Australia's Paddle-Steamer Days

Australia is like no other country in the world. The animals are different. The weather is different. The history is different, too, although pioneer roots and a common English heritage give North Americans and Australians a deep bond.

In real life, most of the earliest settlers didn't want to go to Australia in the first place. They were brought as prisoners from England and Ireland after British prison authorities could no longer use America as their "dumping ground," or the place they could take all the worst prisoners.

In the meantime, gold had been discovered in Australia in 1851. Former prisoners and plenty of new people wanted to get rich quickly, but of course not everyone did. And just like in the American West, gangs of outlaws soon sprang up to rob stagecoaches and banks. In Australia, the people called them "bushrangers," just as they called their woods and backcountry the "bush."

The most famous bushranger was Ned Kelly, a son of Irish immigrants. Though he was eventually caught and hanged for murder when he was only twenty-five, he grew to become a legend, a sort of Australian Robin Hood. Like Robin, he was surely a rebel, but there's no record of him ever giving the money he stole back to the poor.

In the meantime, life was bustling on Australia's largest and most important river, the Murray. Men built paddle-wheel steamboats as quickly as they could out of the eucalyptus, or "red gum," trees that grew around the place called Echuca.

Echuca, an aboriginal word that means "where the waters meet," was the perfect place for a town because two major rivers came together there. The city of Echuca, in fact, soon became known as "the Chicago of Australia," because it was so busy during the 1860s. Many people brought their wool there to be shipped from their ranches, or "stations," downriver to oceangoing ships. The railroad also came to Echuca in the 1860s.

Much of Australia was born here. Like America's Wild West, it was a place for big dreams, where everyone had a chance to make a new life—no matter what their past. And just like the waters of the rivers, it was a place where the people of many different countries met and came together.

This was the world where Becky, Patrick, and Michael continued the search for their father.

From the Author

One of the best parts about writing is hearing back from readers. Do you have any questions or just want to let me know what you thought of the books? Please feel free to drop me a line, care of Bethany House Publishers, 11300 Hampshire Avenue South, Minneapolis, Minnesota, 55438.

Robert Elmer

Series for Middle Graders*
From Bethany House Publishers

ADVENTURES DOWN UNDER · by Robert Elmer
When Patrick McWaid's father is unjustly sent to Australia as a prisoner in 1867, the rest of the family follows, uncovering action-packed mystery along the way.

ADVENTURES OF THE NORTHWOODS · by Lois Walfrid Johnson
Kate O'Connell and her stepbrother Anders encounter mystery and adventure in northwest Wisconsin near the turn of the century.

AN AMERICAN ADVENTURE SERIES · by Lee Roddy
Hildy Corrigan and her family must overcome danger and hardship during the Great Depression as they search for a "forever home."

BLOODHOUNDS, INC. · by Bill Myers
Hilarious, hair-raising suspense follows brother-and-sister detectives Sean and Melissa Hunter in these madcap mysteries with a message.

JOURNEYS TO FAYRAH · by Bill Myers
Join Denise, Nathan, and Josh on amazing journeys as they discover the wonders and lessons of the mystical Kingdom of Fayrah.

MANDIE BOOKS · by Lois Gladys Leppard
With over four million sold, the turn-of-the-century adventures of Mandie and her many friends will keep readers eager for more.

THE RIVERBOAT ADVENTURES · by Lois Walfrid Johnson
Libby Norstad and her friend Caleb face the challenges and risks of working with the Underground Railroad during the mid–1800s.

TRAILBLAZER BOOKS · by Dave and Neta Jackson
Follow the exciting lives of real-life Christian heroes through the eyes of child characters as they share their faith and God's love with others around the world.

THE TWELVE CANDLES CLUB · by Elaine L. Schulte
When four twelve-year-old girls set up a business doing odd jobs and baby-sitting, they find themselves in the midst of wacky adventures and hilarious surprises.

THE YOUNG UNDERGROUND · by Robert Elmer
Peter and Elise Andersen's plots to protect their friends and themselves from Nazi soldiers in World War II Denmark guarantee fast-paced action and suspenseful reads.

*(ages 8–13)